LOCK DOWN

"You have to listen to me!" Archer yelled as the bars closed on his tiny cell. "Walton, you have to listen to me!"

"Or what, Castor?" Walton asked, grinning sadistically. "Or you'll have me fired?"

Walton mumbled a command into his wrist-com, and a wall of steel rolled over the bars, eliminating all light and sound.

Archer collapsed in the darkness. He had never felt more alone. He rubbed his face and was repulsed—he remembered it wasn't his face at all.

FACE/OFF

A Novel by Clark Carlton
Based on the Motion Picture Written by
Mike Werb & Michael Colleary

HarperPrism
A Division of HarperCollins*Publishers*

To Mike and Michael—thanks for saving my face.
—Clark Carlton

HarperPrism
A Division of HarperCollins*Publishers*
10 East 53rd Street, New York, N.Y. 10022-5299

ISBN 0-06-105792-4

HarperCollins®, ®, and HarperPrism™
are trademarks of HarperCollins*Publishers* Inc.

Cover photos courtesy of
Twentieth Century Fox Film Corporation

First printing: July 1997

Printed in the United States of America

Visit HarperPrism on the World Wide Web at
http://www.harpercollins.com

❖10 9 8 7 6 5 4 3 2 1

Chapter 1

"Vincit qui se vincit."
He conquers who conquers himself.

Sean Archer gently kicked his heels in the horse feathers of Pegasus. The beast's wings flapped hard through a sky as blue as a peacock's breast as Sean's son Michael was getting away on his own mount, a flying unicorn. They had disappeared around an ice-cream castle of clouds when Archer heard the silver tinkle of Michael's laughter from deep inside the mists and glimpsed the cherry red balloon clutched in the five year old's hand. Pegasus trotted on invisible steps to where the boy and unicorn rested.

"Come on, Mikey. They won't wait for us," said Archer, grinning at the boy.

"My horsey's hungry," protested Michael, as the unicorn tugged at a tuft of cloud and chewed it with golden teeth.

"He can eat later. Let's go."

Father and son were flying on their steeds

through a cottony canyon when they spied the other riders in pursuit of a flying fox. Boys and girls dressed in red tails and black top hats rode astride a winged sow, a winged lion, a polka-dotted pterodactyl, and a pink elephant using its enormous ears to flap through the air. "Tallyho," said Michael, as he and his father joined in the hunting party.

The flying fox was nowhere to be seen, but Archer bristled when he heard the flapping whir of a helicopter before it tore through a veil of mist. Archer could not see the pilot as the copter hovered before the hunting party. But, squinting, Archer made out a face which, at first, looked like his own. The face resolved into features that ignited a hatred so explosive in Archer, he felt as if his flesh were roasting on the inside. The pilot's face was cold and impassive as he aimed a rifle at Michael.

"Michael!" Archer cried, as he leapt from Pegasus onto the boy's unicorn, jerking the reins from his son. The bullet exploded through the balloon and ripped into Archer's chest. The blast knocked the wind from his lungs, but he kept his arms wrapped around his son as a second shot ripped past them.

"Go! Go!" Archer screamed, jamming his heels hard into the unicorn's belly. The creature swooped down and away, leaving the copter in the distance. When Archer spotted his home, they began a rapid descent. Once on the ground in the backyard, Archer pulled his son to safety inside the house.

Looking out the kitchen window, Archer couldn't see the chopper. Michael's arms were still clasped around his father's neck, and Sean smelled cherry Bubblicious on the boy's breath.

"Daddy, you're bleeding," Michael cried.

"But you're all right," Archer responded, and stroked the boy's hair. Suddenly, the warmth from the boy's body vanished. Archer's son had melted in his arms, then dissolved into thin air. . . .

Overwhelmed with grief, Sean Archer awoke from his dream, the same weird-assed nightmare he had had a thousand times. Breathing hard, he threw his legs over the bed and cupped his face in his hands. He was waking up to the real world, where his son had been dead for eight years.

The real moment of his son's death crashed back into memory—they were in Griffith Park, riding the carousel in the grove of date palms. The carousel had only recently been restored by a preservation society, and "Camptown Races" was tooting "doo-dah, doo-dah" on the calliope. Michael was on the pink unicorn, and Archer was on Pegasus, when a gust of wind tore away the boy's balloon. Michael had tried to grab the string, but he slipped. Archer reached over to grab the boy and had pulled him into his lap, when suddenly gunfire blasted through the music, and the red balloon burst. At first, Sean had felt a slight pain in his upper back, but then it flared into throbbing agony. He was vaguely aware that blood was soaking his shirt.

His only thought had been to shelter his son, but as he reached to engulf him, Archer felt the blood rush from his head, and he slumped to the carousel's deck. Nauseated as the ride kept spinning, Sean had lost consciousness. Struggling to emerge from inky blackness, he had come to and crawled like a crippled insect to the little body on the whirling deck and reached for Michael's tiny hand. The bullet had blasted through Archer and passed into the boy's chest, puncturing his heart and lodging between his ribs.

Blood had drenched the boy's T-shirt, and his already lifeless eyes were turned up and away from his father, as Archer tried to scream for help. Archer collapsed into the sticky red puddle. Before he spiraled downward into a frigid unconsciousness, Archer glimpsed the sniper scrambling through the date palms and into the scrub of the Hollywood Hills.

Eight years later, Archer was shaking at the edge of the bed, trying not to wake his wife. But Eve was already awake, watching her husband through slitted eyes. She knew exactly what he had dreamed and exactly what was going through his mind. And as often as she had seen it, it never failed to evoke her pity. "Sean," she had told him on countless occasions, "you must stop thinking about it. It will never bring him back, no matter how many times you replay it. For your own sake, let it go."

But Archer knew that, as long as his son's murderer was at large, it might never stop. The memory would unspool in his head, as vivid as the day it happened. And each time the memory of that life-defining event returned, it left him sick with guilt. If he'd never taken up with the Feds, had never distinguished himself as an agent, Mikey would still be alive.

Sean rose and looked out the window at a reddish sun ascending in a cloudless sky. He knew it would be a harsh, hot day, a day in which the merciless California sun would drain the life from man, animal, and plant alike. It was the time of El Niño, the days of migraine headaches and dry winds from the south. He was already dressed—he had only meant to lie down for a few minutes before giving in to a jittery slumber. Cursing himself for sleeping as long as he did, he pocketed his FBI badge in the liner pocket of his sweaty suit jacket. Wide-awake and anxious to start the morning, Archer had been tipped off through his network of snitches that the killer of his son had returned to the city of fallen angels.

□ ■ □

The soprano was a lovely blond girl, about seventeen, and the pleats of her choir robe failed to hide her curvaceous hips and bosom. On her way to the water fountain, she passed a man dressed as a priest who made little effort to hide his delight in her bright and beautiful face and what promised to be bountiful mysteries beneath her silky, orange robe.

The man pretending to be a priest was unaware that his disguise was poor. He thought he was dressed as a Catholic, but the full white collar he was wearing belonged to the Episcopalian clergy. The soprano was a Baptist, and unfamiliar with the ways of other sects, but she knew it was odd for a man of the cloth, whatever the particulars of his faith, to swagger the way he did. He suddenly turned on his heels and followed her to the water fountain. She thought it odder still that he would brazenly brush himself against her as she bent over the stingy spurt of the water fountain.

She turned on him, and snapped, "Excuse me, sir!"

The man stared back, unshaken, before his lids lowered, and the faintest of smiles curled on his lips—he was unapologetic about his lust. His brown eyes smoldering, the unflappable man said, "My apologies," as the flustered girl looked into his face.

The soprano was suddenly fascinated and felt pinned by his eyes—they seemed to be pulsing, as they might be were he pumping himself into her. She realized he was not like any clergyman she had ever known, but a man so completely at ease with his every selfish desire that it gave him a powerful sexual appeal and the charisma of a tyrant. Coming to her senses, the girl worked herself out from under his stare and scuttled back to her choir. That morning, two hundred strong, they were singing Handel's *Messiah* in the semifinals of the International Choir competition. She was a soloist.

He thought about following her—it was enough of a challenge to interest him, but the briefcase he clutched in his hand reminded Castor Troy that he had come to the Convention Center to conduct other business. He turned into a service elevator and lowered himself to the basement housing the electrical control center.

Sean Archer would not exceed the speed limit on his way to the office, vigilantly driving at precisely the posted speed until he parked his car in the exact center of his allotted space.

Once he arrived, he realized he had forgotten to urinate, something he had meant to do over two hours ago.

Never one to miss washing his hands, Sean was momentarily shocked when he looked in the mirror and realized that the sallow man looking old before his time was himself. He splashed cold water on the dark bags of his eyes, then chastised himself for his vanity. *Christ, Sean*, he admonished himself. *You don't have time for this.*

He burst into the briefing room, spilling hot coffee on his wrist and staining his last good shirt. The other agents bristled, immediately shot through with Archer's tension. Loomis, the rookie, was glued to his computer screen. Castor Troy's mug shot glowed in the upper right of the screen as his criminal dossier scrolled by endlessly. Loomis was nearly paralyzed by the diversity of Troy's crimes. They began with the torture and decapitation of his neighborhood's cats and dogs, followed by the dousing with gasoline and torching of a rival in love, and the eventual theft of a school bus, which was promptly driven over the cliffs of Malibu. That was when Castor was twelve years old. As a thirteen year old, Castor had graduated to the rape of a geography teacher and the subsequent attempted murder of the vice principal of discipline, who had had the poor judgment to report the crime to the police. The authorities failed at convicting Castor of anything in Juvenile Court. Even as a kid, Castor was known as the Teflon Terror, to whom nothing would stick.

The crimes Castor was suspected of grew more spectacular with each passing year, but he was a brilliant student who breezed through high school and graduated at fifteen. When he entered college, he altered his name slightly, which severed him from his police record. Before graduating from UCLA, Castor was recruited by the CIA. He succeeded in learning all the Agency had to teach him and, once he had defected, went from petty street hood to world-class mercenary.

With impressive contacts culled from the Agency's files, Castor became the man to call for bombings, assassinations, kidnappings, and terrorism for hire. During the ten-year Iran–Iraq war, Troy had performed services for both sides. He had been on the payroll of the Palestine Liberation Organization, Muammar Qaddafi, the IRA, and various warring factions of the Russian, Italian, and Vietnamese *mafias*. It was almost certain he had been hired to murder a Mormon bishop by the leader of a renegade polygamous faction of the Church of Jesus Christ of Latter-Day Saints.

Archer cleared a desk top of soggy take-out cartons to set his coffee down. "Any follow up from the SIS or LAPD Intelligence?"

"No sir, nothing yet," answered Buzz Williams, not removing his eyes from a computer grid map. He had been waiting for over twenty minutes for a download that was just creaking through. Squat and muscular, Buzz looked like a fireplug with a crew cut.

"Call them!" Archer shouted. "*Keep* calling them. What about our airport and bus-terminal teams?"

Wanda Tan already had three parties on hold when she broke from her current conversation. A divorceé and one of the few female agents who was also a mother, she was keenly aware of Sean's agenda when it came to Castor Troy. "Sir," she intoned in a voice more maternal than deferential, "we've had everything from psychics to satellites on this. Even *if* Castor was here, he must have slipped the net by now."

"He's here!" Sean shot back, involuntarily pounding a fist into his open palm. "Don't ask me how I know. I just do. And we're going to keep looking until we find him."

Wanda sighed. She understood, but the rest of the agents silently fumed, as Archer's steely eyes chastised each of them with a brief, burning glance. The last glance fell on Tito Biondi, who kicked away his chair, slammed down his phone, and pressed himself on Archer.

"Step outside, Sean," he urged, lightly pushing Archer out the door.

"Don't push me, Tito."

"Stop pushing *them,*" Tito shot back, jerking his head toward the staff. "You gotta cut them some slack. They've been working around the clock on high alert."

"I'll cut them some slack when I cut myself some slack."

Archer marched out, slamming the door behind him. Tito ran after him, catching up in the corridor. He grabbed Archer by the arm and spun him around. The two men stared at each other, faces grim, bodies poised to strike.

Tito sniffed and wrinkled his nose. "When's the last time you showered, Sean? You're ripe."

Archer exhaled, almost relaxed, and sniffed his pits. *Pyew!* Tito was right.

"How about we send your jacket out for cleaning this morning?" Tito asked, gesturing to Sean to surrender his jacket. "And I think I've got a fresh shirt in my office. Come on."

Looking into his best friend's eyes, Archer sensed the depth of Tito's concern and almost smiled. They turned into Tito's office, which was tastefully decorated in the Spanish Mission style.

□ ■ □

Castor pulled the clear, sticky threads from his glue gun and neatly pressed the modest porcelain box onto stacked cases of explosives set among the vast circuitry. The glue bonded quickly. Castor crushed out his Gitane and thought of lighting a second one, when he heard the quiet shuffle of someone approaching. The janitor, old and slightly hunchbacked, had followed the smoke trail, not in hopes of apprehending the offender, but to bum a cigarette from him. He was surprised to see a priest emerging from behind the security door. He stared at Castor.

"What are you doing, Padre?" he asked in thickly accented English. Castor responded in the Spanish he had learned from one of his women.

"Thank goodness! I feel like Theseus in the labyrinth. Can you kindly show me where the men's room is?"

"Padre, this area is off-limits," the janitor responded. "How did you get in that room?"

Whatever respect Castor's priestly disguise had commanded from the janitor was rapidly disappearing. Castor considered telling him he had sought out a secret place to hide his vice of smoking, but he sensed the old man was already too suspicious. Flopping a priestly arm around the man's shoulders, Castor walked the janitor to the stairwell.

"You know, I'm usually in the position of hearing other people's confessions, but I have one to make to you. I was planting a bomb."

"A bomb?"

"Yeah. You know . . . boom!"

The janitor stared at Castor in disbelief.

"A big explosion. Followed by fire, destruction, carnage . . . oh, never mind."

Castor placed his elbow under the man's shoulder blades and catapulted him down the stairwell. The man was thrown out and over the flight of stairs and landed on his back, his head dangling over a step as he moaned. Castor tripped on the man's bucket and read the name crudely printed on the side: Felix. Castor kicked the mop and bucket down the stairwell, its gray, soapy contents spilling down the steps. He approached Felix, planted a foot on his forehead, and snapped his neck. Castor looked down on what appeared to be an accident as the soprano's choir began a gospel-tinged excerpt from Handel's *Messiah*.

"Father Troy" was passing through the crowd on the main floor, but stopped and listened reverently as he identified the young soprano in the first row, readying for her solo. Even before she looked up, she felt his eyes penetrating her, chilling her to the bone. When her gaze locked with his, she dropped her music, which floated left then right then left again before landing at his feet. He bent slowly, rose, and handed her the sheets, simultaneously pinning her with his eyes. Only the men were singing as he spoke to her.

"I've never enjoyed the *Messiah*. It's overdone. Gilded. Insubstantial melodies glutted with ornamentation. But your voice makes even a hack like Handel seem like a genius." Castor grinned and did the frug for a few bars.

As he swaggered away, her heart fluttered with excitement. She was elbowed by a neighbor and realized she was late on her solo. When she opened her mouth, a short shriek came out before she could find the melody.

Eve removed her latex gloves, then realized her upper arms were sprayed with blood and the foul-smelling sebaceous fluid that had gushed from a benign, bowling ball–sized tumor. As she washed and dressed, Eve guessed the tumor had been swelling for at least five years in a woman who had complained she could never get rid of those last ten pounds.

So much for small victories, Eve thought as

she remembered seeing Sean shake on the edge of the bed that morning. She had tried phoning him before going into surgery. Even as she pulled her cell phone from her purse to try again, she doubted he would take her call. She knew he was once more in pursuit of Castor Troy, but only because Tito had called to inform her. Eve dialed half the number, then hesitated, feeling the blunted mix of anger and exasperation she was almost used to when trying to contact her husband. Out of a sense of responsibility, she finished dialing the rest of the numbers. His secretary picked up on the first ring.

Archer was taking a combination of aspirin, ibuprofen, and acetaminophen, in hopes of mitigating a caffeine-induced headache, when his intercom buzzed.

"Mr. Archer, your wife's calling again."

Archer downed the pills and reached for the line just as Tito burst in. His eyes were bright with excitement.

"Sean, a jet was chartered at Anderson Airfield under the name of Ethan Goddard. Guess who just showed up to pay for it? Pollux Troy."

Not only did Archer forget his wife, but he also forgot to breathe. Blood rushed to his face, and his headache vanished. He bolted from his chair, which rolled and smashed into the wall.

"Scramble the reaction team, Tito. We're moving out. And get one of our people on that plane."

"Done. But there's still no sign of Castor."

"Where one brother goes, the other's sure to follow." His heart pounding as though he were a man in love, Archer tore from his office.

Chapter 2

Castor was almost relaxed in the leather upholstery of the Lexus as Dietrich Hassler drove him to the airport. The blue lights of the runway reflected on Dietrich's shaved head. The lights stretched toward black mountains whose tops were cloaked in the gray clouds of the night sky. Castor was vaguely annoyed with Dietrich, who was wearing an expensive and trendy Richard Tyler jacket, but a cheap grocery-store cologne with a name that implied a wild animal. Below its cheap spice and lime notes, Castor could sniff Dietrich's real smell, a scent redolent of putrid meat and canned sauerkraut. The tailored jacket and expensive tie failed to refine Dietrich's appearance, serving only to accentuate the crudeness he would never overcome. The Lexus pulled in next to a Land Rover as Castor surveyed the airfield. Assured that he was alone, Castor plucked a fat wad of hundreds from his jacket. Dietrich was pleased, but, more than that, he was curious.

"All this for a detonator switch and a ride to the airport, Caz? Who's the mark? You know I won't tell anyone."

"Some dumb fuck who asked too many questions," Castor spit out. He glared at Dietrich, reigniting a hatred that burned below a mild affection. Castor was already out the door when he softened enough to add, "Say hi to your sister for me."

Dietrich grimaced, and his eyes narrowed to tiny slits. "Say 'hi' from you? Not unless I want my ass kicked off my bones. Happy landing—wherever the hell you're going." Dietrich screeched off, relieved to get away. He was always pulled to Castor, fascinated by him, but Dietrich was even happier to leave the man who had been his greatest benefactor.

Castor needed to be with his brother, needed to see the man who completed him as a human being. In his way was a wall of Nordic flesh, Lars and Lunt Lindstrom, two crystal-eyed twins who seemed to communicate telepathically. Bulging with muscles and barely concealed firearms, they parted to reveal Pollux Troy. Like a human hummingbird, Pollux was in constant motion, as skittish as his brother was cool. Even his voice had a high electric hum to it. Castor saw that his brother's shoelace was undone. Automatically, Castor dropped to tie it, something he had done a thousand times before.

"You're twenty-six minutes late," Pollux said, scratching himself in several places. "You had trouble installing that deuterium trigger. I knew I should've gone with you."

Castor's eyes popped open as he finished tying the lace, and he suddenly clutched at his heart. "Oh my God . . ." he gasped.

"What?"

"I . . . I forgot to turn the damn thing on!"

Pollux was stunned; his constant spasms and twitches suddenly halted as his face filled with blood. "You're . . . you're kidding, right?" he spluttered, turning to the Lindstrom brothers. "He's kidding, isn't he?"

Pollux leapt at Castor and clamped his hands around his throat. "Tell me you're fucking kidding!" Pollux screamed.

Easily breaking his brother's grip, Castor's grin gave way to a toothy, smoke-stained smile. "Of course I'm kidding, bro. Everything went fine." Castor dropped his brother's arms and Pollux's usual twitching resumed. He squirmed like a kid as Castor hugged him lovingly. Pollux pushed and turned away, but Castor yanked him back to complete the hug. Pollux knew he wouldn't get away until he succumbed to the embrace and returned it. The Lindstrom twins, embarrassed by this ritual, looked neither at the Troy brothers nor at each other. They had never hugged each other, and never would.

When Pollux was finally allowed to leave his brother's arms, he stomped off toward the jet. "I hate it when you call me 'bro,'" he spit out. Castor smiled in adoration and turned to the Lindstroms.

"Thanks for baby-sitting," he said, and removed two separate wads from his coat pocket. Castor had learned the twins' silent code and knew they resented being treated as a single unit. Each of them was to receive his own payment, but after all these years, neither Castor nor Pollux knew which one was Lars and which one was Lunt.

"Need anything else, boss?" asked either Lunt or Lars.

"Just lay low for a few days until I contact you. Oh . . . and before I forget," said Castor through an oily smile, "stay away from downtown. The inversion layer is going to be pretty thick around the eighteenth." The twins nodded in near unison before pocketing their cash and leaving.

Castor scrambled into the jet and hustled

into the cockpit. "Let's go, let's go, let's go," he exhorted the pilot.

The pilot would have told Castor to take his seat, but since the pilot was being paid a small fortune in cash, he merely shrugged it off. The jet turbines whined as he taxied down the runway.

Castor took his seat and was sinking into the plush upholstery when he sniffed the faint smell of vanilla and gardenia, the high notes of an expensive perfume. He looked at the flight attendant's ankles, which stemmed up to perfectly long and creamy calves, then thighs which knew no equal. His eyes ran up the tailored minidress to a tightly cinched waist and a décolletage which boasted two firm, full, yet natural breasts. Castor Troy could spot silicone a mile away and knew immediately that these were the real thing—they would be hot to his touch. She set down a neat shot of mescal, which Castor downed immediately.

"Welcome aboard," gushed the flight attendant. "Would you like anything else right now?" The words dropped from her rich red lips like diamonds and pearls. She stared deeply, with the hint of a smile on a face rich in dramatic planes. Castor saw it as an approving smile as he looked her over salaciously, then set his sights on her full mouth.

"Hell yes," he answered, and pulled her onto his lap. "It's the only way to fly." She giggled, not minding at all, feeling his palm slide from around her bottom to the front of her thighs.

Pollux looked over at his brother and realized it wouldn't be a dull flight. At some point he would go back to the sleeping compartment and interrupt Castor and the woman. As Pollux removed his clothes, Castor would demand that she accommodate his brother, too.

The flight attendant seemed bothered by the smell of mescal and cigarettes on Castor's breath, but arched her back as his touching advanced. She tossed her hair back, but turned away from him when the plane suddenly slowed. Castor nearly bucked her to the floor as he bolted from his seat, yanked open the cockpit door, and charged in.

"What's wrong?" he asked, peering out the glass.

"Something's on the runway," the pilot answered, screwing up his face, as if it would help him to see what was racing toward them in the dark distance. Suddenly, at the end of the runway, a pair of headlights from a Humvee stabbed through the darkness. Castor's suspicions turned to certainty as the Hummer sped closer.

"Fuck. It's *Archer*."

Within a second, Castor had his gun to the pilot's head. "Go, damn it!" he shouted, nearly gouging the pilot in the temple.

Suddenly Castor heard a deafening blast inside the cockpit and felt the gun jerked from his hand. The glass was unbroken—the bullet had come from behind. Castor turned to see the flight attendant right behind him, her feet planted firmly and a gun smoking from behind her lacquered nails.

"FBI," she shouted. "Throttle down, Captain."

"Bitch," Castor muttered as he elbowed the throttle up.

The jet lurched forward, and Agent Winters stumbled on her medium-heeled shoes. Before she could regain her balance, Pollux leapt at her and tackled her to the floor. She landed on her chin, biting her tongue. Pollux crawled over her and reached for her pistol.

In the Humvee, Tito was seated next to Archer, holding Archer's weapon in his left hand, his own gun aimed at Castor's face. Archer slammed the gas pedal to the floor and the Humvee accelerated toward the jet. Tito eyed Archer, saw the blind determination in his face, and responded by slumping in his seat.

"Sean, you're playing chicken with twenty-six tons of aluminum," he shouted. But Archer was oblivious. Tito prepared to die, and a relic of his religious upbringing returned as he crossed himself and begged the Catholic God for forgiveness. In a matter of seconds, the two hunks of metal would collide.

Archer had no real notion of what he expected to happen, but was jerked back to reality when Castor reached down to the floor and yanked Winters up, shoving her against the cockpit window. He squeezed her neck tightly while holding the gun to her head. He bared his yellow teeth in fearless defiance.

Waves of heat ran up Archer's back, his entire being seared with fear for the victim and disgust for the man who was going to kill her. Archer cut the wheel, just avoiding the jet, and slammed on the brakes, determined not to let Caster claim another victim. The Humvee swerved before skidding, its screech slashing through his ears. Tito choked on the stench of burning rubber, but could see the Federal backup arriving. Archer stood as an FBI chopper attempted a landing in a maelstrom of dust. The jet was still creeping when the dust cleared, and Tito noticed that Archer was gone.

Tito stared in disbelief as the hatch opened on the jet. He saw the blond flag of Winters's hair as Castor battled to push her out. She was bracing herself at the hatch when Castor clamped his hand on her face and blasted a bullet into her side. For a moment, her fingers scraped at the hatch before Castor shoved her onto the tarmac.

Castor smirked at Pollux, who was taking his turn at keeping the pistol to the pilot's head. They laughed as the jet picked up speed, a laugh so harsh and loud it pierced the din of the engine and assaulted the pilot's ears. He wondered if he shouldn't just end the ride since these men would kill him once they had landed safely. Castor saw him hesitate and swatted his head.

"Get it up, *now,*" he screamed in the pilot's ear. Rubbing sweat from his eyes, the pilot shifted the throttle. Castor almost relaxed, sensing freedom, when he heard the sickening sound of a thousand pounds of aluminum being crushed from above. Castor jumped to the hatch and leaned out.

Stunned with disbelief, Castor saw that the helicopter was on top of them, Sean Archer at the controls, his hatred burning like a nuclear fire as he stared unflinchingly into the eyes of his prey. Castor stared back as a freezing contempt swept through him like an arctic blast. He knew he could infuriate Archer at this moment by doing something that wouldn't waste a dime's worth of ammunition—he smiled. And it had the insidious effect he had hoped for as Archer's face grimaced in a deeper rage.

Jerking up his gun, Castor blasted at Archer from the open hatch, his aim made unsteady by the roll of the jet. Archer anticipated the path of the bullets, jerking and weaving as the slugs made spiderwebs of the glass. A bullet grazed Archer's hand, and the helicopter shifted and lurched back.

Castor cackled when he glimpsed the fear in Archer's face. The copter's bubble collided with the cockpit, then blew away, the runners breaking off. The jet was finally lifting.

Castor looked at Pollux, who was staring out the window as the jet's nose tilted upward to the night sky—their escape seemed assured. Suddenly the plane pitched downward, and Castor and Pollux were hurled against the pilot. "Fuck!" Castor screamed. "Fuck, fuck, fuck!" They could hear the screeching skid of the jet's wheels on the tarmac.

"Jesus Christ!" Tito gasped, unsure if what he was seeing at that moment was real. Archer had regained control of the copter and settled it on the jet's tail, riding it. The jet was shifting wildly as the copter played a dangerous game of leapfrog.

Pollux jiggled like molded gelatin when he realized that the plane was fast coming to the end of the runway. The pilot knew what he had to do, but was rattled when a biplane made a sudden descent toward them. The jet pilot's panic compounded as the runway shrank even further. He managed to veer off the tarmac as the biplane barely managed to avoid colliding with the jet. Looking anxiously at Castor and Pollux, he powered down the throttle into thrust reverse.

"What are you doing?" Castor roared, restraining the urge to slam his pistol's butt in the pilot's face.

"You want the fuel tanks to blow? We have to stop," the pilot shouted back, fixing Castor with a hard look before returning to the throttle.

Castor's gun suddenly found its way into the pilot's ear. With no further thought, he pulled the trigger, and blood and brain matter spattered on the instruments. Castor ripped the corpse from the seat and stared at the controls. He could read nothing—the gauges were covered in blood. He tore at the throttle and controls, but none of them responded. The jet pivoted and clipped a parked earthmover, shearing off a wing.

Archer struggled to free the chopper from the tail. He accelerated the whirl of the blades, but the copter remained stuck as the jet jagged out of control, tilting on the side of the remaining wing. A breeze blew, and that tiny bit of air resistance loosened the copter. Archer pulled up, and the blades narrowly missed the approaching hangar.

Castor and Pollux were not so lucky. The jet smashed through the hangar, its walls folding like a pup tent. The brothers were struggling bugs in a beer can as the sides of the jet crushed inward. Its tail stuck comically out of the gaping hole in the wall of the hangar, resembling a dog too big for his house.

A sudden calm fell over Sean Archer as he landed the helicopter. It was the same calm a marathon runner feels when he realizes the finish line is approaching and no one can catch him. It wouldn't slow his pace or alter his determination, but he was allowing himself the luxury of thinking that the victory might be his. When he stepped out of the chopper, he resembled a dulled cop about to write a traffic ticket.

Tito, Wanda, and Buzz led four others in a charge to the hangar's punctured wall, passing Archer, who was the only one to hear the faint click of Castor reloading his weapon. "Get down!" Archer shouted as he crouched. Staccato gunfire blasted through the hangar, creating an ominous echo. The bullets ricocheted off steel beams and reverberated with a terrifying twang. One of them sped past Loomis, tearing off the top of his ear and slicing a bloody path upside his head. Dazed, Loomis fell to the ground. Other agents were far less fortunate.

Castor paused to reload a second time. He glanced down at his brother, who was pinned under the weight of the wreckage. Pollux sliced his palm open as he attempted to use the up-turned metal of the floor for leverage. He tried shinnying from the foot end and screamed when a shard of upturned metal gouged his rib cage. He panicked, knowing he was hopelessly trapped.

Archer rushed into the silent hangar, then fired almost blindly in the jet's direction. He reached Loomis and dragged him behind a fork-lift, then took a moment to survey the damage. He sickened when he counted three dead agents. Breathing deeply, Archer summoned all his concentration.

Pollux was trapped by steel panels bolted to crushed metal beams. Castor tugged, kicked, and yanked at his brother's metal confinement, but his efforts were futile. "Go," Pollux urged him, weakly.

"What?"

"Go . . . don't let them get both of us." It pained Pollux to speak. He could sense that his left lung was punctured.

Castor blanched, and his mouth quivered. He had never imagined a world in which his brother didn't exist. He bent down to kiss Pollux's sweaty forehead. "Wherever they put you, I'll find a way to get you out," Castor said, brushing his brother's hair from his eyes.

Pollux gave the faintest of nods.

Outside the repair facility of the hangar, Archer joined the standing Feds. Tito noticed the faintest twitch in Archer's right hand.

"We got him now, Sean," Tito said.

"That's what you always say," said Archer, as he popped a fresh cartridge in his gun. "Seal it off. I'm going in." Archer headed into the crammed repair facility, which was filled with airplane parts, hydraulic systems, and massive turbine engines. Perhaps he *smelled* that Castor was still alive and making his way out of the jet. Perhaps they were due just one more confrontation. Either way, Archer was sure.

Castor moved nimbly through the jet's wreckage to the rear door. He pushed the door open and dropped fifteen feet to the cement floor. Pain shot through his legs as the impact knocked him off his feet, but he jumped up and skulked back to a faint outline in the wall, correctly guessing it was the rear exit of a wind tunnel in the hangar. He set down his gun when he found the handle, cranked it down, and tried sliding the panel of steel. He was too weak, or perhaps the door was jammed. Castor was trying again when a voice from the dark startled him.

"Turn around," said Archer, appearing between two enormous turbine engines. Separated from an aircraft, the turbines looked like the electric fans of some race of giants. Castor turned gracefully toward Archer.

"Sean, I'm getting a little annoyed by your obsessive need to spoil my fun."

"And how much would your fun net you this time?"

"What's it to you? I declare it. Here I am, back in the States for less than a week . . ."

"You're under arrest," Archer shouted, biting each word. "Incredibly, you still have the right to remain silent . . ."

"Okay, okay, okay," Castor blurted out, as if Archer had been pumping him for a confession he was finally going to make. Castor's arms flailed histrionically as he eyed his pistol and inched closer to it. Archer was not buying into the distraction.

"Sean . . ." Castor began, still calculating, still processing his chances when something finally clicked. "Sean, I've got something going down next Saturday night. It's gonna be worse than anything God ever dumped on the pharaohs."

Listening now, Archer ever so slightly released

the pressure on the trigger as he moved in. "You can tell me all about it," he said, "from the comfort of your prison cell."

Castor gave out with an annoyingly polite giggle, as if condescending to laugh at Archer's pathetic joke. "What're you gonna do with me locked up, Sean? You'll drive your wife and your kid crazy. I bet your daughter is just about ripe now. I bet she's got tits like hothouse tomatoes. What's her name—Janie?"

Ice water was circulating in Archer's veins. His teeth were grinding. The pressure returned to his trigger finger.

"Mention my family once more, and you're dead."

Castor vamped with a travesty of naïveté. "You . . . you can't shoot an unarmed man, Sean. It isn't like you." Blinking his heavily lashed lids, Castor struck a pose that emulated the schmaltzy prints his mother used to hang of alley kittens and lost puppies. Against his will, Archer found himself fascinated by his enemy's weird behavior, fascinated to the point that he hesitated a split moment when Castor's hand reached for his gun, lifted it, and fired.

Scrambling backwards, Archer made it behind the twin turbines and into the wind tunnel's control chamber. He looked down at the test control panel and saw from the monitor lights that the juice was on. Archer flipped a switch—nothing. He tried other switches with the same result. He looked behind him and realized there was only one way out.

Castor gloated when he saw that Archer was trapped in the control chamber. Stalking like a panther, Castor moved in for the kill. His gun was extended before him, and the salty taste of blood was in his mouth. He fired a shot through the glass, and the bullet ricocheted past Archer's ear. Archer jerked back, and his butt landed on the control monitor, which lit up like Las Vegas.

Castor's ears were assaulted by a sudden roar. The twin engines were blasting. Castor dived for the ground to get under the wind, but the churning tornado force swept him up and tossed him across the hangar. With a nauseating thud, he was slapped into the far wall. His body dropped and smacked like meat falling to the kitchen linoleum. Archer turned off the engines and emerged from the wind tunnel to find Tito running toward him.

"Sean, tell me he didn't get away again," Tito puffed. Archer didn't look at Tito. His eyes were fixed on Castor's lifeless body. Tito and Archer walked slowly toward Castor, half-expecting him to jump up, fully armed, to shoot them. Somehow, Castor's mocking smile had survived him, frozen now, below unblinking eyes. For a moment, Archer imagined that those eyes were alive and searching his own, and he repressed a shudder. Just to make sure, he kicked the body deep in its side. No reaction. Tito looked at Archer's face and found it surprisingly blank.

"You okay?" Tito asked.

"Fine," Archer answered. "I . . . I have to take a leak."

What Archer really needed to do was find a private place. When he finally found the men's room, he left the light off, entered a stall, and sat fully clothed on the toilet seat. Certain that no one could hear or see him, Sean Archer collapsed and gave way to a sob. It was followed by another sob, and another after that. As he wiped away tears, he admonished himself. *Christ, Archer, did you just win the Miss America pageant?* It wasn't happiness. It was relief.

The ambulance arrived, and the paramedics scrambled among the victims. Castor Troy was the last one the medics reached. Although his body was still warm to the touch, no life signs were present. But when the paramedic set the mirrored disc of his stethoscope under Castor's frozen grin, the mirror fogged slightly.

Chapter 3

Pollux Troy's vocal cords were shot. He had screamed for an hour as a crew worked to free him with a combination of blowtorches and crowbars. The crew was somewhat less than sensitive to Pollux's wounds, especially after he had labeled them all something that rhymed with "rock chucker." When the blowtorches "missed" and just happened to burn him, Pollux screamed that he and his brother would murder them all, taking blowtorches to their eyes first, and then to their brains once they had the opening. One of the crew looked around for something to gag Pollux with. He thought about his socks, which would have been humiliating, but decided it was a waste of good socks and stuffed an old rag in Pollux's mouth.

Once Pollux was freed, he was heavily manacled. He had finally managed to spit the rag from his mouth. It was kindly returned to Pollux by the donating crew member. "You keep that, buddy," he said, with the fakest of smiles, stuffing it into Pollux's shirt pocket. Only Pollux's head and feet could move. As a result, all his manic energy was channeled to his head, which constantly darted, turned, and bobbed. He was dragged out to a SWAT van, where he half prayed to rejoin his brother. "Where is he?" he panted. "Where's my brother? I need to see my brother!" The van's doors closed on Pollux's desperate pleas, and he was driven away.

Assistant Bureau Chief Victor Lazarro arrived and swelled with an almost Roman pride as he stepped from his Lincoln Continental. He strutted imperiously to Castor's body, the face covered with a sheet, as it was loaded into an ambulance. Lazarro pulled back the sheet for a good look, aware that the focus had turned to him now. He sucked in his gut and turned his good side to the photographers' flashing cameras. A physically imposing man, talk had filtered back to Lazarro that he had grown soft, that too much time had passed since he had brought in a big fish. *Let's see those desk jockeys in DC try to put me out to pasture now,* he thought to himself. Lazarro purposely bulled his way through the gathering media and, knowing they were following him, approached Sean Archer to shake his hand.

"Damn fine work, Sean. You made the entire Bureau look good."

Archer shook his superior's hand weakly, casting his eyes down. He looked at the slain agents and softly funneled his words to Lazarro. "Yeah, it was real fine, Victor. Especially the casualties. Winters, Pincus, Weincoff, and Christianson made everybody look great."

The dead were laid out in a row, waiting to be body-bagged. Sean was still looking at them, counting the number of widows and fatherless children this evening had wrought. Lazarro was instantly deflated and berated himself for his own selfish concerns. A photographer who had stepped over the media cordon worked fast to steal a snapshot of the dead. Lazarro's face went stony. He and Archer were on the photographer immediately. Archer snatched the Nikon from the photographer's hand, ejected the film, and shoved back the camera.

"Classified information," said Lazarro. "No photographs." Jerking his head over his shoulder, Archer signaled for the photographer to leave. Once he had gone, Lazarro saw Archer wander back to the corpses to touch them, to get a final look. And then Archer suddenly slumped, overwhelmed with grief, and doubled over. Putting a caring arm over Archer's shoulder, Lazarro led him away from the media and the carnage.

"You okay, Sean?"

Archer kept eyes to the ground as he nodded.

"Go home. Get some rest. Tell Eve."

He nodded again, looked at Lazarro, and saw that his concern was real. Archer's stomach growled like a grizzly bear, and he realized that it had been hours since he'd eaten. His last meal was an Abba Zabba, a Zagnut, and a paper cup of chicken broth.

Sean sat outside his house, in the driveway, sipping a carton of 1 percent milk. The house, a renovated Craftsman bungalow, looked strange to him. When had the window casings been sanded and repainted? When had the color TV antenna been removed? Had they always had a hummingbird feeder? Did camellias usually bloom this time of year? Why was there a dry patch at the end of the lawn? Was a sprinkler broken?

Archer couldn't get Castor's taunt out of his head. *What're you gonna do with me locked up, Sean? You'll drive your wife and your kid crazy!* One of the marriage counselors they had seen had told Archer that his obsession with Castor Troy was a convenient means of running from his wife and child. Shortly after this theory was presented, Archer rose from his chair and promptly responded that this was all the marriage counseling he needed right now, thank you. Now, as he looked into the windows of his own strangely unfamiliar home, he wondered if that counselor wasn't right. He had had no fear in confronting Castor Troy, arguably one of the most dangerous men in the world when he was alive. But fear was exactly what he was feeling as he finished the milk and prepared to face his family.

Eve was fretting as she sat on the living-room sofa and laced up her running shoes. "Hi," Archer said, and she looked away. He studied her face, a face he usually found as appealing as he had the first time he had seen it. Eve exercised, took vitamins, and looked after herself. But when she was worried, her forehead was divided by a large crease, and her usually sensual lips looked thin and colorless.

"What's wrong,?" he asked.

Eve nodded toward the kitchen. Archer could see his daughter's feet at the breakfast table. She was wearing what she called Skechers. To Archer it looked like an army boot. As a child, he remembered lobbing the familiar insult at classmates, "Hey, your mother wears army boots." Now young women were wearing them proudly, in conjunction with lace and velvet. For some time he had suspected that his daughter had tattoos on the most intimate parts of her body, and now he could see one on her upper thigh. It was a wreath of roses around a marijuana leaf.

The tattoo wasn't surprising, but the red cartons of Marlboro cigarettes piled on the dinette were very unexpected. Eve spoke in a voice dredged in exasperation. "Jamie complemented her D in history with an F in shoplifting. When the police came, she . . . she stole their squad car."

"*What?*"

Archer marched into the kitchen and saw that the cartons had come from a crate. "Stealing cigarettes?" he asked, staring at her and realizing she was wearing black lipstick on her upper lip and red on the lower. "Are you trying to get arrested *and* give yourself lung cancer at the same time?"

"That's right, father figure. Don't even ask me what happened."

"How did you steal a squad car?"

"I didn't steal it. I just borrowed it for my big escape. Stupid cop left his keys in the ignition. Everyone thinks I'm so cool now."

Jamie stood, matter-of-factly poured herself a cup of coffee, and folded her arms. Archer hated it when his daughter called him "father figure." He had no idea what to say and looked to Eve for help. She shook her head and turned away from him—he would have to figure this out himself. Jamie slitted her eyes and thrust her two-toned lips forward in a pout.

"Okay," said Archer, after exhaling. "What exactly happened?"

"Like you'd ever fucking believe me!" Jamie shrieked, bolting from the room. Anticipating her, Eve calmly opened the door as Jamie whizzed past, closing it when she was gone.

"Okay. You tried, Sean," Eve said. "You failed miserably, but you tried."

"Everything I say is wrong. I can't talk to her anymore. She gets money, right, in case she wanted to *buy* cigarettes?"

"She doesn't want to buy them. She wants to steal them. She's acting out."

"Of course she's acting up."

"No. Not up. *Out*. She won't tell us what she's feeling, so she's presenting it dramatically. She's frustrated and angry, and she wants us to know how she feels by implanting those feelings in us."

"Well, she's a brilliant actress. Someone should give her an Oscar."

Eve looked into Archer's face, puffy with fatigue. "I know you're busy, Sean, but can we please make time for some family counseling?"

"I thought you were taking her."

"We *both* have to go. Please? Before she needs a parole officer? I can't take all the responsibility for this. I can't take any of it, really."

"Are you holding me responsible?"

"Yes, as a matter of fact, I am."

Eve picked up her medical bag and mechanically kissed her husband on the cheek. "Gotta go. I've got patients waiting. Walk me out, and I'll give you this week's highlights."

Archer drew a long, tremulous breath through his nose. "Eve . . . we need to talk." Eve, not hearing him, was already on her way out. She counted out the litany of events on her fingers.

"The freezer died on the first, followed by Jamie's iguana on the second. The burial was on the third, followed by the exhumation on the fourth, and the delivery of the corpse to a taxidermist. Finished product is expected to arrive on the eighth. On the fifth, you missed our scheduled Date Night. The remains of what would have been a romantic dinner are in the refrigerator, including half of a homemade Nesselrode pie. I gave your ticket for *Beauty and the Beast* to Jamie and suspect she liked it even though she threatened to barf over the balcony several times. Your mother called *you* on *her* birthday and . . ."

Archer felt her words like an assault. Had their relationship become nothing more than a list she rattled off during their brief encounters? He grabbed Eve firmly and stared into her eyes. She knew enough not to be frightened, but suddenly her heart was pounding.

"What . . . what is it, Sean?"

He tried to speak, but the words reached his tongue, only to slide back and away to some black and distant place. He cocked his head with a look that was touchingly pleading. Eve gathered from the look on his face that something dark and frozen was finally unthawing. She glimpsed the sunny, carefree man her husband had been when they were first dating, the one who was so damn cute.

"Is it . . . is it him?" she whispered, daring to hope it was true. "You finally got him? It's . . . it's over?"

Sean could barely nod. An avalanche of emotions rushed over his face. He was dizzy, feeling as if the planet Jupiter had lifted from his shoulders, and he was free, floating into space. He looked up and realized how much he loved Eve, realized he was finally sharing this moment with the one person who knew every inch of his pain. He also realized that her relief was, like his, stained by the sad-sweet memory of their baby son.

Eve pulled him close. For a moment, Archer imagined she was larger than him, her arms a sheltering embrace for them both. Their bodies burned against each other before Archer found his words. "I'm going to make everything up to you and Jamie. I'll put in for a desk job. We'll go back to that counselor. This time, I mean it."

Eve knew he was sincere when she felt the splash of his tears on her neck. She had never imagined feeling that.

He should have wanted sleep, but Archer found himself blaringly awake. In the shower he noticed that the few chest hairs congregating around his nipples were turning gray, like his sideburns. Eventually, when he was more gray than not, someone would make the mistake of saying it made him look distinguished. The truth was everyone his age was going gray, and there was nothing distinguished about it. Maybe he would ask Eve to buy him some of that Grecian urn stuff, or whatever it was called. He couldn't buy it himself. Should he apply it to his chest, too? He plucked one of the distinguished gray hairs from his chest and watched it get swept away in the stream of water. Curiouser and curiouser, this world without Castor Troy. He was Archer in Wonderland.

He was surprised to find a closet full of freshly laundered shirts, no starch, hung on hangers. Eve was just as busy as he was—where had she found time for that and Nesselrode pie? Like his house, his wife seemed like something of a stranger. Or perhaps he was just rediscovering her. The shower had freshened his skin, and the bags under his eyes had vanished. A good workout with some time on the StairMaster, and he would be his handsome self.

Jamie lay on the bed, fully clothed. She also was reacting to something strange, the sound of whistling. She had no idea what tune her father was attempting, but was sure that whatever it was, he was butchering it. Archer was actually less than conscious that he was whistling the Carpenters' "Top of the World" when he passed his daughter's room. She appeared to be out cold. Her bed was covered in layers of carelessly arranged clothes, most of them black or polyester prints: the seventies retro look. He paused to look around this forbidden place and noticed that her dresser vanity was covered with uncapped lipsticks and a large box with over forty shades of eye shadow. He figured the waxy black pencil next to a sharpener was what gave her those spidery eyelashes.

Her stuffed animals were still on the shelves but gathering dust. Googums, a pink elephant, had lost the luster of his black plastic eyes. He remembered how she used to clutch Googums, and, using her little arm, pretend it was a trunk to ask for peanut M&M's. That same little girl had a tattoo now. Couldn't she have waited a little longer before she grew up? Archer quietly stepped in, cleared a few things to free her blanket, and pulled it up to her chin. The instant he left, Jamie kicked the blanket off.

When she knew her father had gone, Jamie ran to the kitchen and lit a cigarette. She inhaled the Marlboro's bitter perfume, felt dizzy, and told herself she liked it.

After Archer parked his mid-sized Oldsmobile sedan, he looked up at the FBI building and noticed that they had repainted the Bureau's seal. He anticipated that today would be different, a day of celebration and acknowledgment, but the sensation he felt most strongly at the moment was emptiness. By the time he reached the checkpoint, a vague depression had settled over him. Eddie, the security guard, slouched on his stool.

Archer was mystified as to how Eddie held his pants up. His soft, aged body was like a rotting pear stilted on toothpicks, with his pants just barely rising over the top of his thighs—they did not come up over his overflowing buttocks. Perhaps his shirt was pinned to the inside of his pants. His scalp and neck were covered with wens. Tufts of white hairs grew between the wens, as weeds do between stones. Who had the pleasure of giving this man a haircut? His mouth stank of salmon salad and cigarettes, and his voice was full of gravel when he barked, "Print, please, Mr. Archer."

Archer pressed his thumb to a scan-pad. The monitor blinked from red to green, and he was cleared. Why, Archer asked himself, was he so distressed by the physical state of the security guard?

The bullpen was as efficient as a beehive, each drone set to his task. Agents, cryptologists, and their support staff buzzed at their routines. Archer strode somewhat stiffly in his dark Brooks Brothers suit, drawing congratulatory nods and thumbs-ups. A few had the urge to rise and shake his hand, but Archer had always been distant, and his demeanor today was almost a rebuff. When he reached his office, his team was gathered outside. They were smiling, and Tito began the applause. It tapered off rapidly when Archer failed to return their smiles.

"Much appreciated," Archer deadpanned. "Now, let's get back to work, please?" Archer vanished into his office, but left the door open.

Buzz stared in disappointment at Archer's back, and Wanda rolled her eyes. "Is that stick ever going to fall out of his ass?" she whispered.

"What stick?" Buzz replied. "I thought it was a telephone pole, myself." Unknown to either of them, Archer heard their words and was saddened. Didn't they understand what he'd been through? What the apprehension of Castor had cost in human lives?

Kimberly Brewster was the office's acknowledged sexual presence. She was the woman who the other ones took notice of every morning, as she somehow managed to wear something different nearly every day of the year. Men usually failed to notice her outfits, but they never failed to notice what was underneath them. Even standing still, she jiggled. Her torso was a chiffonier with the top drawer pulled out. Kimberly needed little makeup on her naturally lovely face. Her bright green eyes twinkled from frames of long black lashes. She entered Archer's office as he booted up his computer. In one hand Kimberly held her boss's messages, in the other was a magnum of Perrier Jouet champagne.

"Telegrams, Mr. Archer. Notices of congratulations. And the CIA sent this over. What should I do with it?"

She hoped he would ask her to chill it for

some celebration at the end of the day. Archer saw the label, realized it was an expensive bottle, and returned to his computer screen. "Send it back, Miss Brewster, and tell them I said to stop wasting the taxpayers' money. My money. Your money. Anything else?"

She thought about telling him to dunk the bottle in Vaseline and shove it up his very tight ass. Instead she replied, "No, sir."

Wanda was passing as Kimberly left the office. Both of them shrugged shoulders. "Four years—and he's still calling me 'Miss Brewster,'" she said.

Archer *had* noticed Kimberly's shapely backside, clad in a short cream-colored skirt. But he had sneaked a cursory glance from the corner of his eyes, and only after her face was completely turned from him. Kimberly had always wondered if Archer's wife was one of those incredibly fortunate women whose husband's attention never drifts far from home, or if she was some sad celibate married to a sexless workaholic. She would probably bet on the latter.

Her boss returned to his computer screen and scrolled through Castor's file. Archer grimly contemplated an endless series of faces, all of them Castor's victims. The first was the president of an East European nation, the second a Venezuelan oil executive, his wife, and their three children. One was the madam of a Nevada brothel who had attempted a takeover of the other houses.

The next series of victims were young, beautiful, blond women, all of them listed as missing. They were authentically blond, not bleached, because they were being "exported" to the *harims* of wealthy Arab oil sheiks. One of the survivors, Cynthia Van Duzer, was actually a brunette. When her purchaser, the overweight potentate of a renegade sub-Saharan sheikdom, learned that a series of bottles were needed to sustain her image, he threw her unceremoniously from his Mercedes and into the desert, where she nearly died of thirst. She was rescued by Bedouin shepherds, who delivered her to a party of German geologists in search of natural gas.

Cynthia found her way back to the United States, and Sean Archer was assigned to investigate her story. She told him about a man named Jeremy LaGarde. She described LaGarde as charming, seductive, and brilliant at lovemaking, though his lengthy sessions in bed were suffused with some darker energy, and more than a tinge of sadism. LaGarde had wealthy, influential friends, who threw lavish parties in expensive hotel rooms. He was friendly with Cynthia's modeling agent, some film producers, and a reputedly untouchable coke dealer.

Archer had realized almost immediately that LaGarde and Castor Troy were the same person. Sean had already been fascinated with Castor, who was a true genius of crime. It was as if Castor had set himself the task of outdoing the world's worst criminals in multiple categories. To great acclaim within the Bureau, the young Agent Archer broke Castor's sexual slavery ring. A series of indictments sent Troy and his associates scurrying deep underground. The humiliation of Castor was completed when Archer uncovered and expropriated the vast network of holdings under Castor's multiple pseudonyms and fictitious corporations. In absentia, the Troy brothers were convicted of tax evasion, drug trafficking, and a myriad of other crimes. It was at that time that some of Archer's fellow agents had remarked to him that he physically resembled Castor. Archer had learned to think like his enemy and could unravel his past and predict his future. Castor Troy had become just as obsessed with Archer, obsessed with extinguishing his life.

Archer was now viewing the last image in the file, the slain five-year-old son of a young FBI agent. Archer had been a less than religious man after his son's death, and he had strong doubts about the existence of an afterlife. He was even more skeptical of the notion that the dead could return to this plane. But as Archer typed CASE CLOSED and waited to trash the file, he spoke to his son with the hope that Michael could hear him. "I got him, Mikey. I got him for you," he whispered.

Archer pressed ENTER, and the file vanished into the mainframe. An emptiness as vast as the universe expanded inside Archer. He looked away from his monitor and around at his office in mild surprise. His office had been decorated in Early American by Tito's housemate, but the shelves and art objects were completely obscured by curling photographs, yellowing newsclips, and clues and totems of Mr. Castor Troy. For the first time, Archer was seeing it all as clutter, as an accumulation, as a detritus-ridden monument to his obsession. Had he never noticed it before? Curiouser and curiouser.

All of it could go now. He walked to one shelf and immediately filled his wastebasket. It would take several large GLAD bags. The thought of it all sitting in black plastic bags in a garbage bin awaiting incineration was unbearable. Archer tried to bury those feelings as he looked at the emptying shelves, but it was particularly difficult to squelch the faintly expanding notion that in ridding his life of Castor Troy, he had extinguished a part of himself. The emptiness gnawed at every part of his being, and he panicked when he realized he had no idea how to fill the cancerous void. "*Work,*" he told himself. *"Throw yourself into work."* A stack of photos fell to the floor, floating like autumn leaves.

Tito stood outside Archer's door, silent for a moment, as he watched his friend bend over. Tito could remember when he had envied Archer's physique. As Tito looked at Archer, the sight was a reminder of past glories. Archer had talked about going back to the gym. Maybe Tito could actually get him to go. He knocked on the open door.

"Sean?"

When Archer turned, Tito could see what looked like despair before Archer could don the mask. For his part, Archer was relieved his friend had come to distract him.

"What's the news, Tito?"

"The good news is Loomis is going to be okay. He needs some surgery, but they say they can get him a new ear."

"Wow. What's the bad news?"

"Brodie and Miller from Special Ops need to see you."

"I don't have time for those cloak-and-dagger guys," Archer retorted, turning back to his housecleaning.

"You better make time, Sean," boomed a profoundly deep voice. Archer turned to see all three hundred pounds of Ned Brodie charging into his office like a rhinoceros. At his side was Hollis Miller, a sinewy, athletic female with a clean-cut face more boyishly handsome than pretty. She held up a disc and spoke in husky tones.

"We found this in the jet wreckage—among Pollux Troy's effects. If you'll allow me . . ."

Archer signaled for her to take a seat. Soon, a CAD schematic of Castor's bomb glowed on the computer screen. Hollis scrolled through the second page. Archer's eyes dilated, and he wondered if the others could hear his heart thumping in his chest. "Porcelain casing . . . thermal cloak . . . undetectable payload."

He stared blankly at the monitor, and muttered, "Worse than anything God ever dumped on the pharaohs."

"What?" Hollis asked.

"It's what Castor said to me before he died. He . . . he wasn't lying."

As Archer explained his remark further, Tito wasn't sure if Archer had actually turned green, or if his skin was discolored by the screen's glow. Sometime later, Archer realized that the awful emptiness had vanished. The weight of Jupiter was on his back again, yet in some part of that nearly unbearable burden there was something strangely comforting, something that made him feel whole again.

Chapter 4

One of the interrogating agents wished that deodorant was dispersed among prisoners because Pollux Troy stank like maggot-ridden pastrami. He was wired to a state-of-the-art polygraph, which measured not only his respiration and blood pressure, but voice modulation and stress-induced variations in the electrical conductivity of his skin. Pollux was already sweating heavily before he was wired to the machine, which precluded a fifth measurement for perspiration. One interrogator suspected correctly that Pollux's stench was a result of eating an extremely specific diet that altered his blood and skin chemistry and thus confounded their instruments. Since his incarceration, Pollux was subsisting on coagulated bacon grease and raw carrots. He was getting an extraordinary amount of iron from sucking on rusty nails and licking the yard's chain link.

On a monitor in his office, Archer, Lazarro, and the FBI brass watched Pollux's inquisition. From the panicky shifting of his eyes, he seemed to be on the run. But the measurements of the polygraph, which were feeding into Archer's computer monitor, were eerily steady.

"Tell us about the bomb again," said Thomas "Torquemada" Fuchs, a seasoned veteran at tripping up the coolest of criminals.

"I told you seven times now," Pollux moaned in his most nervous and nasal voice. "That bomb was just a crossword puzzle to me. A mental exercise. I get bored sometimes. I never built the fucking thing."

Archer and Lazarro looked at the computer screen—again no change. Lazarro shrugged his shoulders and turned off the monitor. Archer stood his ground, looked into Lazarro's eyes, and said, "He's lying."

"Sean, he's hooked up to a full-spectrum polygraph that no one's ever beaten."

"He's manipulating it. Pollux Troy is a brilliant sociopath. Don't ask me how, but he defeated that machine before he was even hooked to it. That bomb has been built, and it's going to detonate on the eighteenth."

"How do you know?"

"I just do."

Lazarro shook his head, sighed through his nose. "I trust your instincts, Sean. I always have. But there's nothing we can do without some concrete evidence."

Archer looked at the rest of the brass, who gave deferential nods to Lazarro. Archer wanted to shake them, scream at them, let them know how right he was. The pain of his anguish felt like a demon child within. He remembered when Eve was giving birth and he was her coach at Lamaze classes. To deal with the pain, you had to breathe slowly and deeply. Inhale, exhale. Inhale, exhale. The brass heard his deep breathing as he stomped out of his own office.

Archer tramped to the granite wall of the Bureau's Memorial. He had seen the engraver working on the wall and shuddered, knowing that four new stars were being added to the existing ones, all of them commemorating members of the Bureau whose lives had been sacrificed in the line of duty. One was for Pincus, one for Christianson, the others for Winters and Weincoff. Would there be more stars on the wall if the bomb squad accidentally detonated Castor's plant? Would the city of Los Angeles lose ten thousand lives? What could

Archer possibly do about it? Lost in his thoughts, he was unaware he was being studied by two approaching figures. He turned to see Brodie and Miller, sure from the look on their faces that they had an agenda.

"Get some coffee, Sean?" Miller asked.

"No, thanks."

"How about something to eat?"

Archer did not respond and sank back into his worries.

"Didn't Castor give you any clue as to where this bomb might be?"

"One person knows, Ned. His brother Pollux. And he'll keep his mouth shut until it blows."

Brodie shrugged his massive shoulders. "We could plant an agent in his cell—get him to spill the location."

"Where's he incarcerated?"

"Erewhon," said Brodie. "Luckily enough, we've got enough convictions on both the Troys to put them away for life." Brodie had named the supersecret high-security prison where the nation's most dangerous criminals were kept. Few people knew of the prison's actual location, though Archer had heard a rumor that Erewhon was either in the remote mountains of Colorado or in an obscure desert of California.

"No point to it," Archer said. "Pollux Troy is

a textbook paranoid. The only man he would ever talk to about that bomb is Castor himself. And dead men don't talk."

Brodie and Miller exchanged a knowing, somewhat guilty look. "Sean, there might be a way around that," Miller said.

Archer was vaguely alarmed. And very intrigued.

"We can arrange for you to enter Erewhon Prison as Castor Troy," said Brodie, as he and Miller led Archer through Tartarus, the clandestine underground complex situated in a labyrinth of tunnels well below the Bureau's complex. Archer's ears needed popping because of the sudden change in pressure from taking a five-minute elevator ride that sank for miles. He made Brodie repeat himself. "You heard him right the first time," Miller said.

Sean felt suddenly nervous and alert and remembered that the artificial atmosphere of Tartarus was pumped full of oxygen. "Why not send in the tooth fairy?" Archer mocked. "Maybe Pollux talks in his sleep."

Brodie and Miller exchanged a second knowing glance as she puffed on a Camel Light. Archer followed them into an intensive-care unit, where a flaccid, yellowish body lay as limp as an old carrot. Tubes and hoses were plugged into every orifice. One tube suddenly constricted as a flow of bright yellow urine ran to a floor sink and trickled away. The three of them turned to each other, Brodie and Miller smiling, and Archer blinking in confusion.

Hesitant at first, Archer got closer to the body. On an unconscious level, he had already smelled who it was. Now his eyes had to confirm it. The tubes obscured the face, but the tattoos were unmistakable.

"Why are you keeping him alive?" Archer asked. "As long as he's breathing, he's dangerous."

"Relax, Sean. He's a vegetable," said Miller as she took her cigarette and ground it out on of Castor Troy's left leg. The flesh blistered, and a smell vaguely reminiscent of barbecue filled the air. The leg did not flinch. Archer was mildly aware that he was comparing himself to Troy's naked body, and he noticed that they were similarly built. Archer realized they had been similarly muscled before he had given his diet over to fast food. The biggest difference was body hair—Archer was smooth, but Castor was covered with a wiry growth.

"We can give you the ultimate disguise, Sean. Literally give you the face of Castor Troy," Brodie said.

"You're crazy," Archer scoffed.

"Your friends aren't as crazy as they appear, Mr. Archer. They just have all the facts," said a middle-aged figure on Rollerblades as he skated into the room. He was sipping a Big Gulp full of Mountain Dew and listening to *Abba's Greatest Hits* on his Walkman. A long braid of silver hair trailed down the back of his T-shirt, imprinted with the Hot Wheels logo. He extended his hand, and Archer noticed his watch, a cheap digital with the Mr. Bubble logo. "I'm Malcolm Walsh. I run the Physiological Camouflage Unit for Special Ops."

"I know who you are," Archer deadpanned.

"But you don't know what he can do," said Miller. "Physical augmentation, enhancement surgery . . ."

"He can disguise a compromised agent or alter the likeness of a government witness," said Brodie. "Even change his voice and his handwriting."

"More snitches have disappeared in here than in the East River," said Miller, with a grin.

"Please, you're embarrassing me," Walsh said, biting into a Tootsie Roll. "Let's just show him how it's done."

Walsh skated away. Archer followed him to a large aquarium, where white rats were scurrying in cedar chips. All of them had strange bumps growing from their backs, like ships' sails or lumpy pyramids. On closer examination, some of those growths looked like ears and noses. One rat had nothing on his back but a recent incision.

"That's Pee Wee," said Walsh, pointing to the freshly stitched rat. "We excised his growth for today's operation. I think you'll recognize our patient, Sean."

They followed Walsh to an observation booth over the surgical bay. Archer saw Loomis the Rookie on the surgeon's table, with eyes closed and mouth wide-open, drooling. The surgeon was gingerly scraping at the charred flesh around the ear that Castor had shot off. A technician nearby watched closely as the pins of a strange machine rotated in opposite directions, pulling and shaping a freshly grown sheet of human skin.

"What is that?" Archer asked.

"A derma-grafter," Walsh replied. He pulled a bag of BBQ Fritos from his fanny pack and opened them. The derma-grafter was snugly fitting the skin over cartilage grown in the exact shape of a human ear. When it was completed, the surgeon lifted it, cut away the excess skin, and compared it to Loomis's intact ear. They were identical in shape, but the new ear was a pinkish white.

The surgeon placed the ear, adjusted it several times after calibrating the exact location in millimeters, and began suturing. Archer looked at the huge monitor screen on the far wall. The sutures had become invisible within minutes. As the ear filled with blood, its color normalized. "Will the fake one feel different?" Archer asked, as Walsh offered corn chips.

"Nothing's fake, Sean. It's completely organic. The sutures are made of a living gelatin derived from human bones—they'll be completely integrated in an hour. With the anti-inflammatories available to us now, your agent will wake up unable to remember just which ear he lost."

Walsh skated into a neighboring laboratory, signaling Archer and the others to follow. "Your situation," Walsh said while rolling backward, "should you choose to do this mission, would be a little less permanent. And a lot more classified."

Walsh picked up a face-sized organic shell from a series of prototypes. It was made of murky yellow cartilage and resembled dust-covered beeswax. Layered over the shell were striated bumps, identically formed and symmetrically located on both sides of the cartilage. Walsh handed it to Archer, who pressed it to his face like a mask. A lump over the cheekbone fell to the floor. "This'll fool Pollux," Archer scoffed, flipping the shell back in its place. He folded his arms over his chest.

Walsh picked up the fallen lump, pressed it back into place, and held up the shell. "This is a state-of-the-art morphogenetic template, Mr. Archer. The inside can be built to match the exact shape of your skull; the outside, exactly like Castor Troy's. Then we fit his face right on top . . ."

"And you become him," said Miller. She was grinning at the notion. The smell of corn chips was making Archer mildly nauseated. Walsh might have been a genius, but he hadn't mastered the art of chewing with his mouth closed.

"Are you talking about *taking* the guy's face?" Archer asked.

"Borrowing, Sean" answered Brodie in a low boom. "The procedure is completely reversible."

"One way or the other, the mission ends on the eighteenth," added Miller. She hadn't stopped smiling. Walsh handed Archer the shell a second time. Archer felt his blood racing. He needed to defecate . . . soon. As he turned the shell over and over in his hands, it seemed to take on a golden, luminous quality. He imagined himself with the face of Castor Troy and was strangely electrified. "Now that I have all the facts," Archer said, "let me reiterate. You are all *crazy*."

Brodie could see that Archer's lips were curling in the faintest of smiles. And his eyes were bright—the pupils were dilated, twinkling under the fluorescent light. A further push in the right direction, and Archer would agree. "Sean, you know Castor better than anyone. You've lived and breathed him for years."

"And you're the only one who can pull this off in time," Miller added.

Suddenly it seemed completely absurd. "No," said Archer emphatically. "Absolutely not. How do I get out of here?" He paced around the room like a captive wolf.

"Listen to us," Miller said. "The facts of this bomb point to huge devastation. We're talking about ten thousand lives, maybe more."

Leaning into a corner, Archer mopped sweat from his brow with his sleeve. Brodie walked over, spoke in a hush.

"Sean. We know that when your son died you made a vow never to let Castor Troy take another life. You tried but failed. Now is your chance to fulfill that vow."

"You son of a . . ." Archer's voice broke off. He realized immediately that Brodie had been in the psychologist's files. No one but the Bureau's shrink had known he'd taken a vow. Deeply sickened, Archer pushed past them with the blankest expression and ran out the door.

"I don't think that went very well," Walsh whispered.

"Trust me," Brodie said. "He'll be back."

Archer searched for the men's room. Once in the booth, he wasn't sure if he should drop his trousers or fall to his knees since he was throwing up on both ends.

It was easy for Archer to come up with a complete list of Castor Troy's associates. Within twenty-four hours, all of them had been gathered up, flown in, or dragged down to the Bureau for questioning.

Fitch Newton was dressed like Mr. Rogers in a cashmere cardigan. He straightened his tie as he denied his association with Troy. "What kind of sick superfreak do you think I am?" he spluttered at Tito. "Sure, I used to fraternize with Mr. Troy; he was quite amusing at cocktail parties and shared my interest in gardening. That's how we met, you know, at an orchid show in Santa Barbara. He was very knowledgeable about orchids, don't you know, and particularly fond of anything with a white throat and long, showy stamen. He detested orchids that were fuchsia-colored or had crenellated beards. It was an absolute shock to me and my wife, don't you realize, when we discovered he was a wanted *criminal* . . ."

Tito and Archer rolled their eyes in disbelief. They had no doubt that Newton had been supplying Castor with an arsenal of weapons for the past ten years. The Bureau had strong suspicions that Newton and Castor had sold a cache of plutonium to Pakistan. But after relentless questioning, all Fitch would admit to selling Castor Troy was a swarm of bees for an apiary.

Aldo "Snow" Andino had low heavy lids over his eyes and sported black leather even on the hottest days. He wore his leather under the hot lights, and when he began to sweat, unzipped to reveal he was shirtless underneath. In the early eighties, he had enjoyed a certain celebrity in Hollywood because he vended cocaine of unquestionable purity to stars and film executives. Andino had avoided being busted for years, and part of his invincibility was due to being completely free of his own product. Blood tests showed only that he was taking Xanax, which a doctor had prescribed for depression. Now he had a smaller clientele, which included Castor Troy, a man he would only admit to having met. Hard as diamonds, he deflected all of Archer's questions for two hours, answering only yes or no. When he stood to shake out the sweat which had condensed inside his jacket, he finally said, "I have four little words for you *Schutzstaffels*: ACLU."

Besides being an occasional chauffeur to Castor Troy, Dietrich Hassler was practically an institution at Santa Anita and Hollywood Park: he was a fixer and responsible for some of the greatest upsets in racing history. Unassuming Oaxacan stable workers, *Indios* who barely spoke Spanish, much less English, were on his payroll. They were adept at cleanly drawing and discarding a few quarts of blood from the favored horses hours before the race. It wasn't often that Dietrich could put in the fix, but when he could, Castor Troy had benefited. Dietrich operated from an art gallery on Rodeo Drive. Smugly unflappable, he rose at the end of the interrogation and pressed business cards on Archer and Tito. "Hope I've been helpful. I've just acquired some absolutely fabulous Lichtenstein serigraphs. Come down to my gallery, and I'll set you boys up. My God, it's hot in here."

Dietrich snapped open a Japanese fan when his clutch was returned to him. He fanned himself dramatically as he exited, covering his mouth and looking coy.

"Model citizens all," Archer said, turning off the lights and collapsing into a seat. "Why was Hassler behaving like such a . . . such a. . ."

"Big queen?" Tito finished for him.

"Yeah."

Tito grimaced. "It's his way of getting back at me."

"Getting back at *you*?"

"He knows I play the pork clarinet."

"You *what*?"

"You know. I munch the veiny burrito."

"The veiny burrito?"

"Christ, Sean. That I take it in the face."

"Oh." Archer was silenced, then he almost grinned. "Well, if you ask me, his impression was almost too good. And I thought it took one to know one."

"Well, he isn't." Tito looked at the "guest list."

"Who's next?" Archer asked.

"Her. She's the last," said Tito, motioning to a booth where a woman sat, holding a little boy in her lap. She had the high, dramatic cheekbones of a fashion model and the widely spaced eyes of a doe. But her clothes were definitely last year's news, even a few years before that. Her lovely face resembled a Slavic Madonna portrait with its downturned mouth, the face of someone with a deep and mysterious wound.

"It's Dietrich's sister, Sasha Hassler," said Tito. "She and Castor were an item for a while."

"I know all about Miss Hassler. I've busted her enough times."

Archer watched her as she held flat the corner of a coloring book so her son could use his Crayolas. Her son, Adam, like all five-year-old boys, reminded Archer of Michael. Archer stuffed down the punctured feeling that association brought and entered the booth.

Sasha's eyes flashed, and her chin jutted when she saw Archer. He could almost feel her hatred, piercing him like a hundred needles. For a moment, she thought she saw something soft in Archer's face when he looked at her boy. "What do you want?" she spit out, her eyes returning to the coloring book. Adam offered her the red, and she absently colored.

"When was the last time you saw Castor Troy?"

"Who cares?" she answered. "He's dead." She looked briefly at Archer, her features drawing angrily to the middle of her face.

"Answer the question."

Sasha turned completely to Archer. "Look, I'm clean. I teach art to kids now. I . . ."

"You're also still on probation."

Fucking asshole, she thought. *He would bring that up.* She set her son down and crossed her arms. Archer could see he had reached her and went on the attack. He looked in her face, then at her son, and said, "Miss Hassler, would you like your son put in a foster home?"

She lunged at him. Her fingernails went for his face. She wanted to gouge his lips off. Archer grabbed her wrists and held firm.

"Sure, you son of a bitch! Tear his life apart in the name of the law! That's how you cowards operate."

Archer was as frozen as a glacier. He cocked

his head slightly, his face softening almost imperceptibly, as somewhere in the recesses of his mind he imagined the trauma of her being separated from her son. She sensed his vague sympathy when he spoke in a quieter tone. "When was the last time you saw Castor Troy?"

She looked him directly in the face, and answered, "I haven't seen him for years." He considered believing her. Sean suddenly looked at the boy, realizing he had been clinging to Archer's pants leg. Adam was bravely attempting not to cry but failing. "Don't hurt Mommy, Mister," he sobbed, and Archer was stunned. The boy wondered why men were always hurting his mother. He had decided that men were bad, and he wouldn't grow up to be one.

"I won't hurt her," Archer replied. When he felt the fight ebbing from Sasha, he loosened the grip on her wrists, and she backed away.

Sasha fell to her knees and hugged her son protectively. Archer's face was stony, but a storm of sorrow rained hard on his heart.

Archer had left without telling Tito where he was going or when he was coming back. Speeding east on the freeway, Archer absentmindedly found himself on the I-15 to Las Vegas. He was thinking about gambling. He was a hundred miles outside the city when he reached the desert full of rock piles, spiny Joshua trees, and mountains seared and cracked by the sun. He stopped to urinate.

Standing in the sand, he made a goal of trying to soak the entire surface of a rock with his piss. A whitish scorpion emerged from under the rock, its claws before it, its tail glistening with urine as it curled up and over the thorax. Ants scurried between a dead hare and their nest, fearless as they climbed under or over the scorpion in their path. Archer jumped back in his car and returned to the city. Just where the hell had he been going?

He was circling Castor's hairy, muscular body, overcome by doubts again. Miller and Brodie had explained several times how the complete transformation would be achieved, showing him miraculous before-and-after pictures of other procedures. By the time Sean had circled the body for the eighteenth time, he was convinced it was the only thing to do. He flinched somewhat when he lifted the oxygen mask on Castor's face and saw that his signature smirk had been cemented into place. Brodie and Miller stood by patiently.

"What about Lazarro?" Archer asked. "Did he really approve this?"

"No way. We can't tell him," Brodie answered. "The red tape alone would take a month. This is a top-secret operation. Completely off the books. We'll have to do it at Walsh's own lab."

"We know you're close to Tito," Miller said. "If you need him, he can help you prepare. But you can't tell anyone else. Not Lazarro, not your wife, not your mother. Nobody."

Archer didn't like that part. It seemed extreme, overly cautious. The doubts returned like a swarm of locusts. The three agents were silent. All they could hear was the hum of the life-support system and the loud tick of the wall clock; to Archer, the seconds suddenly seemed like goose steps to a horrible explosion and mass murder. He nodded his head, almost imperceptibly, and turned to his partners.

"All right. I'm in."

Miller's tensed body suddenly loosened. She realized she hadn't been breathing. Brodie patted Archer on the shoulder. "Go home and get some rest, Sean. Tomorrow you'll be a new man." Archer took one last look at Castor Troy, lifting his left eyelid and looking into the glassy orb. No, he wasn't looking back.

Chapter 5

As Archer stepped out of his car, the neighboring boys' basketball rolled into his driveway. "Yo, Mr. Archer. Over here!" shouted the lanky teenager standing under a rim bolted to a telephone pole. Archer picked up the basketball to take a shot. Stiffer than rigor mortis, he was virtually incapable of bending his knees, lowering his butt, and shooting the ball with the tips of his fingers. The ball barely arched under the basket and bounced into the yard opposite. "Sorry," he said, shrugging.

Archer entered his house and heard loud, pounding music with a scraping guitar and earsplitting feedback. He went to Jamie's room, concerned for her hearing. He raised his knuckles to knock, then decided against it. Entering the master bedroom, he saw Eve in bed, and closed the door behind him. Her arms were clasped around a pillow. Her back curved softly down to a tush he was still crazy about after all these years. He felt a pleasantly heavy affection for her as he sat on the bed to study her face, her wavy blond hair, her thin and elegant neck. How peaceful she looked, and for a moment, how peaceful he felt. From under her eyelids, he saw movement, and realized she was dreaming. She clutched at the pillow in her arms and Sean shook her awake.

"Eve? Eve, wake up."

"Sean? Oh, Sean." Her head fell into his lap, and she was comforted. "I was having a nightmare."

"What about?"

"You. You were falling. You had a parachute, but it wouldn't open."

Archer paused. "Were you there to catch me?"

"No."

"How come?"

"I don't know. . . maybe it's because you never need my help."

Archer lifted her from under her arms, turned her face, and kissed her. She kissed him back, hard. His fingers ran forcefully down her back. Unable to tear her hungry mouth from his equally demanding one, she slipped her hands inside his shirt and dragged her nails lightly across his tensing flesh, excited that the "drought" was finally ending. Her heart was rapidly thumping in surrender as her fingers paused over the thick, round scar near his heart.

Eve felt him spasm, then tense. She looked in his face, which was suddenly impassive. She knew that look, and knew it meant the opposite of indifference. Archer collapsed on the bed and turned away from her. She wrapped an arm around him.

"It's all right, Sean."

He stared at the ceiling fan. He couldn't look at her.

"After all these years, I still can't get it out of my head . . . an inch to the left and Mikey would still be alive."

"And you wouldn't be." She tried to look him in the eyes, but he wouldn't take them away from the slow whir of the fan. The pain festering under his stoic detachment suddenly suffused her being. She was weak and shaking as she mustered a hopeful tone. "Things will get better now that you're home, Sean. Everything's going to be okay, now that . . . that man is finally out of our lives."

"Eve . . ." Archer began, and backed off. Deep within him, Archer felt steel coils twisting to the breaking point. He was tempted to tell her the whole truth but fought back the urge. "Honey, if I had to so something to find some closure . . . I should do it, shouldn't I? No matter how crazy?"

Eve folded her arms. The crease was back in her forehead, separating her eyes into two cold and glassy orbs. "Oh, God, Sean—you're not going on assignment again?"

The words of the marriage counselor throbbed in her head: repetition compulsion, intimacy conflict, obsessive behavior. Archer rested his hand on her stomach. "One last time, Eve. While I'm gone, I want you and Jamie to go to your mother's in Santa Fe. It's important . . ."

"You said you'd be here," she shouted at him. "You promised! What could be more important than that?"

"I can't tell you. I can't, except . . . only I can do this."

She sat up, a tempest gathering in her flashing eyes. "You want me to tell you it's okay to leave? Okay, go on! Go!" she shrieked. Archer turned and stared at her.

"I said GET OUT!" she screeched, and in a fury of sobs, she pushed Archer out of bed. He fell on his ass and banged his tailbone. She turned away from him, clutching her pillow, returning to the position in which he had found her minutes ago.

He pondered sleeping on the couch—there was an afghan he could use—but his thoughts turned to the door at the end of the hall. The door to Mikey's room was always left slightly open, just like when he was alive. He had been scared of sleeping with a closed door, convinced that if ghosts or monsters could enter through his window, his father could rescue him through the door. Sean flipped on the Bert and Ernie lamp by the bed and turned back the Batman bed sheets. He looked around the room, as neat and tidy as a museum exhibit, and felt his ring finger itching. He toyed with his wedding band and realized it would have to come off tomorrow.

Sean tweaked Ernie's nose, and the light went out. His legs were too long for the mattress, and he suspected he wouldn't get much sleep that night. Up on the ceiling, plastic stars and planets glowed a pleasant, faintly eerie green. Sean remembered that Christmas afternoon when he had stood on a ladder with a wad of sticky putty, pressing the stars to the paint. The stars would look random to Michael that night. But once he learned the alphabet, he would know his name had been written by his father into the heavens themselves.

□ ■ □

Other lights were glowing, too. The crimson LED of the bomb timer counted down in hermetic silence in its box inside the Convention Center. Outside the main hall, a failing fluorescent tube flickered inside the marquee. Tomorrow, the letters on the sign would be changed to read WELCOME AMERICAN BAR ASSOCIATION.

Shell-shocked, Tito sat with Archer on the Metro-rail as it clipped smoothly through a tube under Long Beach Harbor. "This is fucking insane, Sean. Who convinced you to do this? Turning yourself into another person? Especially *him?*" Tito downed his breakfast, a pineapple doughnut and a can of Diet Coke. "We don't even know where Erewhon Prison is." As Archer sifted through Castor's dossier, his photos throughout the years spilled to the floor.

"We have no choice, Tito. It has to be done." Archer looked through the pages of Castor's history again, a pointless exercise since he already had it memorized. Lights flickered as the train slowed. Tito realized they were under the ocean when he looked out and saw frogmen emerging from a service bay, their wet suits glistening under the yellow light. They were reporting to a crew captain supervising tunnel repairs.

Antsy, Tito thumped his leg. He rose to face Archer, grabbing on to a pole. "You haven't got a chance in hell of fooling Pollux Troy. Castor drank, smoked, and walked around with a twenty-four-hour hard-on. He was nothing like you." Tito turned away from Archer, then dramatically spun around and threw his Coke can. Archer caught it easily and wagged it. "What gives?"

"That was wrong, Sean."

"What?"

"Castor Troy is left-handed."

Archer looked at the can in his right hand. "Don't worry. I'll do my homework. If Walsh can do half of what he claims, I'll get Pollux to talk." Tito sighed, and returned to his seat, resigning himself to Archer's decision. Archer was fiddling with his wedding ring. When he yanked it off, he saw the white skin underneath—that was something they would have to change, too.

"I need you to hold on to something" Archer said, as he passed Tito his wedding band. Tito grinned and recalled the last time he had held that ring, as best man at Archer's wedding. Tito pocketed the band, and when he once again looked at his friend's face, he saw for a moment that Archer was afraid.

"It's okay, Sean," Tito said, his warmth and concern quite evident. "It'll work out." Archer's silent gaze spoke volumes about his trust and affection for his friend.

Outside a battered ranch house and a collapsing barn, Holstein cattle grazed on dusty weeds. Archer and Tito were squeezed into the cab of a Ford truck as it arrived at the ranch. The Mexican driver, dressed in jeans, a flannel shirt, and a straw cowboy hat, pulled into the barn, where there were no animals. Malcolm Walsh stood waiting for them. No Rollerblades, but he was wearing a Wonder Woman T-shirt and sucking on a fresh Big Gulp and a Charms cherry lollipop. "Over here, boys," he shouted, waving them over. They joined him on a metal platform that sank inside the earth to an antechamber.

Walsh breathed into a tube which recognized his DNA fragments, and a large circular door slid open. Archer and Tito followed him through a long, white corridor. Hollis Miller was sneaking a few puffs off a cigarette, which she hastily crushed as the others entered the surgical bay. Brodie was dealing with his anxiety by munching on corn nuts. A video technician made adjustments to his cameras, whose feed went to two giant wall screens. Archer looked up on the wall and saw a greatly magnified electronic image of Castor Troy's inert body. Sean suppressed waves of nausea.

"Take your clothes off, Sean," said Walsh.

"What?" Archer was transfixed.

"We need you to undress."

Archer looked at Miller. She shrugged her shoulders. "It's nothing I haven't seen before, Sean."

Once Sean was naked, Miller never looked at him because the male body vaguely sickened her. Archer was standing with hands folded over his privates when he felt terry cloth over his shoulders—Tito had found him a robe.

Deeply grateful, Archer tied it on. He wandered over to Castor's body. It had lost little of its tone and taut muscularity. Walsh approached Archer. "Shall we walk through it, Sean?"

Archer nodded.

Walsh noisily sucked the dregs of his soda. "Your blood types are different, but there's nothing we can do about that. The height difference is negligible, within half an inch. The feet are close enough. Penis size, when flaccid, essentially the same—average."

"What difference does it make?" Archer asked. "No one's going to see it."

"You're going to prison, Sean. Everyone's going to see it. Castor only has one testicle, so we'll have to pull one of yours."

"*What?*" Archer gasped, and involuntarily covered himself.

"Just kidding," Walsh said, and winked. Archer did not laugh, but he saw Tito and Brodie chuckling in the observation booth. Hollis Miller turned away to light a Camel.

Like a livestock inspector, Walsh poked his fingers into Archer's love handles. "What do you say to an abdominoplasty?"

"An abdomino—what?"

"A tummy tuck," Walsh answered, grinning. "On the house."

"Do it," said Archer.

"Good. I'll do it in a way that your musculatures will match up perfectly."

Walsh looked at Archer's chest and then right into his eyes. "This has to go," he said, touching the scar of the bullet wound. Archer felt his stomach plummet when Walsh got a call on his cellular.

"Hi, sugarpuss," he said, and grinned. His wife was calling him from the ranch house nearby. Archer watched Walsh talk with her and thought they must have a happy marriage. "Pecan pie? Can you save it for me?" Walsh asked. "I'll be tied up for the next twenty-four hours. . . . We'll eat it in bed." Shamelessly, Walsh made kissy noises. "Love you, too. Bye."

A nurse approached to take Archer's robe. An anesthesiologist wheeled out her apparatus, and Archer reclined on the sheetless table. His head was set in a morphing pillow, which solidified, making his head comfortable but immobile. The cushion on the surgical table had the same property, feeling like a water bed at first, but firming up to keep his body rock steady. When the mask lowered over his face, the sharp smell of enflurane mixed with oxygen flooded his nostrils and reminded him of the oil refineries of Elizabeth, New Jersey. As a boy, he used to visit a cousin in Elizabeth to swim in their Doughboy pool. Archer thought he was in that pool now, the cool water lapping at him from inside a sky-blue plastic liner. The water became a whirlpool as his brain fogged—he felt like his head was revolving on a record player as the world around him went spinning. Before he drifted off, he imagined he was looking up at Eve, who was performing the surgery. "I love you, honey," he started to say, but his tongue had turned to thickening Elmer's glue. Everything went black.

Two massive sensors linked to each other in a computer mainframe began rolling on a track above the exposed bodies of Sean Archer and Castor Troy. The sensors were a complex of tiny video cameras, absorbing information in a matter similar to an insect's eyes. They would roll again and again after each separate procedure until their data were matched to within fractions of each other. When it came to the face transfer, Walsh would make no incisions himself. He would let a laser scalpel make them once the exact positions had been determined by the computer. A mild adjustment to the flesh would have to be made for the eye sockets, which could not be altered and were different by a few millimeters.

The easy parts were performed by assistants while Walsh examined his data. Archer's body looked even more similar to Castor's after it was siphoned of its adipose tissues in the obliques, abdominals, thighs, and buttocks. Walsh used a new method which avoided postsurgical bruising by applying a fine laser around the treated areas, which cauterized the surrounding capillaries. He had no problems with re-creating Castor's multiple tattoos—the challenge was using the right color inks to make them look faded. He started with the Great Sphinx, which he re-created on Archer's thigh, then went on to the Hanging Gardens of Babylon. Walsh tsk-tsked at the next of the Seven Wonders of the Ancient World: the Colossus of Rhodes, which was drawn incorrectly, with a Roman toga instead of a Greek tunic.

Changing the eyes was next. Walsh plunged microneedles into thirty-eight separate sections of Archer's irises, washing them from blue to brown. The individual muscles of the iris that radiated from the pupil had to be dyed varying shades of yellowish brown, and a flaw, a blackish greenish speck in the shape of an apple, had to be added to the left eye. Walsh's assistant quietly worked on Archer's fingerprints. The skin around the fingers had been peeled back and treated with a concentrate of retinoic acid that mildly burned them and made them susceptible to grafting. Small sheets of Archer's own skin imprinted with Castor's prints bonded immediately.

Hair was relatively simple, but tedious. Each of the 42,436 chest hairs currently growing on Castor's body had been determined and programmed into an implanter—it quietly hummed as it plugged hairs in an identical pattern onto Archer's chest. Turning to Archer's scalp, Walsh used a laser to cauterize the follicles until he had Castor's receding hairline. A few snips here and there and Archer sported Castor's Roman-senator look.

"And now," Walsh said, as he compared the two bodies, "let's see if I missed anything before I get my hands really dirty." The assistants gathered around the bodies and nodded their consensus. Some differences in muscle, hand, and foot shape were discernible after study, but for practical purposes, the two bodies were substantially identical.

In the observation deck, Tito, Miller, and Brodie were fascinated when the cobalt beams of lasers made identical, simultaneous cuts in the two faces. Miller smirked and was reminded of pie dough when Walsh gently peeled, then lifted, Archer's face from his skull by the ears. Tito stumbled out of the room and vomited into the pot of a coffeemaker.

Walsh set Archer's face in a bath of artificial blood inside a Plexiglas vacuum cube. The blood was circulated every five minutes, spilling in a gentle sheet over the side of the bath to a filtering machine, where it was purified and returned. An assistant opened the cube and, using a high-resolution computer image, located the largest veins and arteries of the face and attached them to a network of fine tubes, which also circulated to the purifier. Archer's pale features suddenly firmed when the secondary pump was turned on—the severed face had eyes of bright artificial blood.

Walsh secured the template to Archer's skull, then turned to Castor and lifted his face. Everyone was fascinated to watch what looked like the drooping mask of tragedy suddenly fit into perfect place and flush pink. So fascinated was Walsh's staff that all of them failed to see that Castor's eyes were wildly twitching in their exposed sockets. His consistent EEG reading had radically spiked. Castor Troy had briefly dreamed that his face had been ripped from his skull. And moments later, he briefly woke from that dream to find it was true. The immense shock sent him back into a coma, and his EEG reading returned to its previous level.

Chapter 6

Archer emerged from the anesthesia with a head full of melted chewing gum. A male nurse sitting in the room reading *Men's Fitness* heard Archer moan. "Welcome back, Mr. Archer," the nurse said. "I'll go and get Dr. Walsh." Archer could not remember where he was. Had he had an accident? Where was Eve? Where was Jamie?

Sean heard Walsh approaching on his Rollerblades, and the sound was strangely terrifying. He half remembered electing to submit to surgery, but could not recall what procedure had been performed. He was fighting panic, suddenly aware that his face was hot and sweaty under gauze bandages.

"Sit up, Sean," Walsh instructed, "and hold your head still." The gauze was being cut away.

"Here we go," Walsh said, his face filled with wonder at his own accomplishment. He pointed Archer to a mirror over the sink. Archer sat up and looked at his reflection.

Archer had left Wonderland. As he stared at the face of Castor Troy, he had gone through a Looking Glass darkly. He pawed at the mirror's reflection. And then he screamed.

"Sean, what's the matter?" Walsh shouted, as Archer banged his fist into the mirror. The mirror trembled but did not break. Archer lifted the night stand by its legs and hurled it into the mirror. Again it did not break. Archer stared at his enemy's face an d blinked. Enraged and panicked, he hammered the mirror with the nightstand until the glass fragmented. Now there were fifty images of Castor Troy before the shards crashed to the floor.

"I'll kill them!" Archer shouted as he remembered everything.

"What are you screaming about, Sean?"

"Brodie and Miller! I'll kill them!"

Archer had picked up a shard of the mirror to examine himself again. Walsh was frightened to see Archer suddenly grip the shard like a dagger.

"Sean, get ahold of yourself!" Walsh commanded. "Do you want me to sedate you?" Archer was crawling on the floor, crying like a baby. Humiliated by his behavior, Archer finally regained control of himself, his pride bringing him around. Walsh and the nurse lifted Archer from the floor and sat him on the bed.

"I'm sorry," he managed between short breaths. "I'm very sorry. I'm okay." Walsh managed to smile and gave Sean a paternal pat on the back.

"I know you are. We have to do your dental work later today. It'll take a couple of hours to do the bonding and to color the teeth with tobacco stains." Archer looked down and studied his flat stomach and hairy chest. The bullet wound was gone. He was speechless as Tito, Brodie, and Miller entered the room. Instinctively, Tito grabbed for his holster.

"It's me, Tito. It's Sean."

Tito laughed at his mistake.

"It worked," Archer said, aware of a slight ache in his throat. "Except for my voice. I still sound like me."

Walsh prodded Archer's Adam's apple. "I implanted a larynx moderator. It seems in place. It'll take a little practice once I activate its microchip. Drink this," he said, thrusting a warm Styrofoam cup into Archer's hand. "It'll bring you right back."

"What is it?"

"Chock Full o'Nuts. With cream and sugar."

□ ■ □

Following the activation of the chip and the dental bonding, Archer's voice immediately made a rapid conversion. The protruding arch of his bonded teeth affected the way his tongue formed consonants. By directing his voice toward his nasal cavity, mildly slurring and keeping his pitch up, he sounded exactly like his enemy.

Other aspects of Castor Troy were not so easy to master. Archer drank wine on special occasions, but he never drank liquor. Now he had to throw back jiggers of mescal, Castor's favorite drink, and he nearly retched in the process. It tasted like shoe polish, and he couldn't help but shudder as it burned down his throat. One drink of it made him woozy, two made him drunk. He wouldn't have time to build a tolerance.

Archer was mildly contemptuous of cigarette smokers, and secondary smoke gave him headaches. Now, on Tito's advice, he was lighting a new cigarette every fifteen minutes. When he practiced smoking in the mirror, he attempted Castor's icy, killer glare. At first Sean simply puffed on the cigarettes until Brodie laughed and showed him how to inhale. It weakened Archer and made him want to vomit.

How, Archer asked himself, did anyone ever get hooked on this? He had started with Marlboro Lights, which were difficult enough, but when Tito pushed Archer to Gitanes, he couldn't stop coughing.

Naturally, Archer preferred his own appearance. As Castor Troy, he was irritated at the amount of hair loss he had to endure for the next few days. The other problem was the hair on his chest. He had caught it in the zipper of his sweatshirt several times, and found sleeping on his stomach to be an itchy experience.

Left-handedness was still the greatest challenge. Though Walsh had adjusted the tendons in his left wrist and finger to enable him eventually to write like Castor Troy, Archer could barely manage a signature that didn't look like a child's first scrawls. When Tito surprised him by suddenly throwing an object, his left arm flew up automatically. But he hadn't switched all activity to the left yet. He had to think about using his left hand to hold his fork when he ate.

No one, including Archer, felt he was ready. But the time had come. He was fretfully packing his bag when Brodie entered his room. "I just called Lazarro and let him know that Castor Troy has emerged from his coma and needs to be incarcerated. We've got seventy-two hours."

"Okay."

"You won't be needing that," Brodie said, pointing to the bag. "The Federal Penal System will now be providing for your every need. Would you mind facing the wall?"

Brodie cuffed Archer, who almost laughed as he was read his rights. They passed through the surgical bay where Castor Troy's body was still sustained by life support. Mercifully, someone had covered the faceless head with a soft plastic mask of protoplasmic liquid. The lidless eyeballs poked up through the mask and every thirty seconds, a machine misted artificial tears over them.

Sean stopped over Castor's body and asked Brodie to lift the mask. Castor's skinned skull reminded Brodie of Lon Chaney in the original silent version of *Phantom of the Opera.* To Archer, Troy looked like one of Michael's old toys: Skeletor, archenemy of He-Man.

"Don't they burn the trash around here?" Archer asked, meaning Castor's body.

"Not until they harvest the organs," Brodie answered. "His retinas are going to be donated to a little girl who's waited five months to have her sight restored."

Archer felt almost happy. In death, Castor would finally make a contribution to humanity.

□ ■ □

Like an angry wasp, a black helicopter dropped from a cloudy sky to the FBI heliport. Armed agents took their positions around the square. Archer watched as a second squad marched out, led by a puffed-up and pleased-as-punch Lazarro. Into their midst, Tito escorted a heavily manacled "Castor Troy."

"You're on, pal," Tito murmured. "If you're not out of there in three days, I'm going to Lazarro."

"I'll be out."

The two men stole a brief, conspiratorial glance as two armed agents approached.

"Watch this hard case, gentlemen," Tito said to the agents. "He'll bite your balls off if he gets the chance." Tito pushed Archer hard toward the agents. Archer tripped over his leg irons and realized Tito was prompting him.

"Goddamn fuck-pig," Archer bellowed at Tito. "You don't have any balls."

Archer resisted the agents and had to be muscled into the chopper. Tito said a prayer as the door slammed shut and the helicopter buzzed into the sky. Archer's heart was beating in time with the blades' violent rotations. One agent rechecked Archer's chains. He was a young redhead with jug ears and splotchy freckles. He reminded Archer of that guy who was always on the cover of *Mad* magazine.

"Don't forget," Archer said, mustering one of Castor's killer glares. "I ordered a kosher meal." Alfred E. Neuman smiled to reveal the split between his teeth, then smashed his elbow deep into Archer's gut. Another agent rolled a hood over Archer's head. When an injector jabbed sharply into his thigh, he spasmed and sagged unconscious.

On the observation deck of the balcony above the helipad, Archer's team watched the chopper get smaller. "What a week for Archer to go on a training mission," said Loomis, as he wandered back to his office. "Shouldn't we let him know?"

"Forget it. He left strict orders not to be tracked down," said Wanda, as they drifted past Brodie and Miller.

"So far, so good," Miller whispered, lighting a fresh cigarette off the butt of another. Brodie just sighed.

Too much death, Archer thought, as he emerged from unconsciousness. For the second time in a week, he had been plunged into a dark and dreamless void which was more like death than sleep. In sleep, one was alive and dreaming—the blind could see again, the crippled could walk, and humans could fly. In the drugged state from which he was emerging, he felt like someone escaping a dark and silent vacuum, terrified at the notion of having to return there. Life of any kind was preferable, even the nightmare to which he was waking up.

He couldn't quite see yet, but had vague impressions of orange-clad men shoving him into a bluish cubicle. He collapsed on a hard, steel floor and banged his head. The clatter of his manacles rattled his ears as the metal gouged his wrists and ankles.

In what might have been as close as a few feet, or as far as a mile away, he made out an orange figure. It was straddling what could have been an elephant's trunk. In actuality, it was the head guard with a water cannon. He was incongruously named Red Walton since he had blond hair. Walton was a large and sallow figure with no lips on his grimly drawn face. He was aiming the water cannon at Archer. "Stand up," he growled.

Archer made every effort to rise, but was too weak. "Stand up!" Walton repeated, but Archer collapsed to the floor. Walton loosed the cannon on Archer's face. The liquid blasted under his chin and threw him headfirst into the wall. He turned from the blast to breathe and got a mouth full of delousing spray. Retching and gasping, Archer was finally awake. He was thrown a pair of heavy metal boots with strange clasps and complexly patterned soles. Each boot must have weighed ten pounds.

"Put 'em on," he was commanded. Archer stood over the boots, attempting to figure out what they were. He looked at the soles and saw sensors of some kind. Inside, he saw soft plastic pads that might have covered circuitry.

"Don't sniff 'em, you perv. Just put them on and stand up," Walton commanded. Archer rose and stuffed his feet inside the boots. Instantly, they cinched tight around his feet, and the clasps wrapped hard around his ankles.

"They're too tight," Archer croaked out.

"So's a noose. Now keep your mouth shut."

Archer lifted his feet and felt like he was trudging on Jupiter.

"Those are lockdown boots," Walton said. "They let us know where you are at every minute, every second of the day. Get out of line, and we'll lock you down." Walton spoke into a wrist communicator. "Lock down twenty-two forty-six," he said. Inside the boots, Archer felt a mild current of electricity that glued them to the floor's powerful magnetic field. Walton lifted a long, orange stick from a holster, dangling like a rapier at his side. He shoved the blunted tip into Archer's thigh. Archer tried to step back, but the boots wouldn't budge from the floor. He screamed and fell as a high-voltage shock ran through him.

"Get up!" Walton bellowed, and jabbed the stick into Archer's chest. He jerked at the second shock, and struggled to rise, barely able to breathe. A second guard, a Filipino, entered with battery-powered scissors. He sheared away Archer's clothes as Walton ranted.

"You are now an Erewhon inmate—a citizen of nowhere. Human rights zealots, the Geneva Convention, and the PC police have no authority here. When I say your ass belongs to me, I mean it. Bend over."

Archer stood naked and terrified as Walton brandished the shock stick. Archer bent over . . . and thought of England. "Reach for your toes!" Walton commanded. Archer heard the snap of a rubber glove being pulled on and braced himself for an examination. *Inhale, exhale* he commanded himself as Walton gave him more than a "once-over."

"Twenty-two forty-six to Security," Walton barked into the wrist-com. In an instant, Archer felt the boots lose their magnetic grip, and he could move. The Filipino threw a jumpsuit at him. It had large black-and-white stripes, like the convict suits of old. The door of the cubicle blasted open, and Archer was marched down a windowless corridor.

The walls and floors were the same steely gray. Xenon tubes in the ceiling cast a harsh white light that hurt his eyes. They reached the checkpoint, where Archer glimpsed the broad windows of Security Central. It was a vast circular room where prison guards in their orange suits and green ties sat in comfortable chairs before monitors with multidimensional graphics of every space in the prison. The prisoners were represented by white circles, with their black identification numbers visible in the middle. Sean gathered from the chain of white circles on the monitors that the prisoners were being herded to General Population.

Walton grabbed Archer's hand and pressed his thumb to an electronic panel. A graphic of Castor Troy emerged next to the thumbprint, positively identifying him. "Twenty-two forty-six to General Population," Walton said into his wrist-com. Turning to Archer, his lipless mouth stretched into a slash of a smile. "I've got fifty bucks says you're dead by dinner, Castor. Don't disappoint me."

A door blasted open, and Archer was pushed into a corridor lined with low, narrow cells. Inside each of them was a thin metallic toilet that thrust from the wall's molding, a toilet he later learned would flush only once a day, automatically, in the mornings. The only other object was a steel table, also a part of the molding. Wait, that wasn't a table, Archer realized, that was the bed. He saw his own cell, number 2246. He passed an orange-suited guard who pointed his shock stick toward the end of the corridor, where lunch, the only meal of the day, was being served.

Archer was prodded to the end of the service line. He picked up a tray and was given two plates. One was full of large gray cubes that were soft, lukewarm, and salty. The second plate was smaller and contained several hard cubes that were vaguely sweet.

"What is this?" Archer asked the server, a fat man wearing an eye patch. On his cheek was a tattoo of an eagle clutching a swastika.

"It's lobster thermidor, sweetie."

Archer glared at the man. "Where's the silver? The napkins?"

"Silver?" The man cackled. "Napkins?" The man kept laughing and served the next prisoner. Archer was handed a metallic cup filled with water. The cup's lip was thick and rounded. Like everything in Erewhon, it had no sharp edges, nothing the prisoners could use to make a shiv.

As he turned into the main dining area, the buzz of the inmates' conversation came to a rapid halt. Every eye turned to him. All Archer could hear was the lone tap of his boots on the floor and the constant hum of the magnetic field. Conscious that he was being stared at, he kicked into a performance and became Castor Troy. Swaggering as much as the boots allowed him, he scowled as he searched among the tables for Pollux. When he didn't see him, he took a seat, a hard metal disc attached to the table by a rounded beam of steel.

Archer watched the prisoners eating with their fingers and did as the Romans. The gray stuff was probably tofu and tasted like nothing. Infused in its slightly bitter aftertaste was probably a tranquilizing drug of some kind. A huge man with a scraggly beard and nearly green teeth stared daggers at Archer, who pretended to ignore him. Who was he and how had Castor Troy fucked him over?

A goateed man with port-wine stains on his forehead turned to Archer. The stains resembled a map of New Zealand and he spoke with a raspy French-Canadian accent. Archer was glad to have someone else to pay attention to besides Green Teeth.

"*Zut alors*! Castor Troy! Remember me?" asked New Zealand. The goatee was new, but Archer looked at the wine stains, at the place where the Cook Strait separated the two main islands, and remembered who was addressing him.

"Fabrice Voisine . . . sure. I . . ."

Archer caught himself.

". . . I believe you got busted by Sean Archer after poisoning five members of the Canadian parliament. Caesar's Palace—in Atlantic City."

"Those English-speaking scumbags should never 'ave voted against the Quebeçois. We 'eard you got wasted."

Archer realized the other inmates were listening to every word. "Do I look wasted, you Queeby fuck-wad?"

Fabrice was rattled. He didn't want any enemies in Erewhon, particularly Castor Troy, who he suspected would soon be running the prison's rackets, scant as they were in Erewhon.

"No. You look *fantastique,* Castor. Really. 'Ere—I 'ave sometheeng for you." From the inside of his jumpsuit, Fabrice produced a rare commodity, a baby-food jar full of booze. Archer figured the prisoners got it from certain guards in return for sexual favors.

"Mescal, Castor. Even 'as the worm."

Archer eyed the green corpse of a worm in the urine-colored liquid. His stomach sank, but he knew everyone was waiting. He downed it, grinned, and chewed on the worm. "Hit the spot," he said, and stuck his tongue out with the worm pulp at the end. Fabrice and the others were laughing as Archer barely controlled his urge to puke. Green Teeth suddenly provided a helpful distraction when he leapt on Archer and started pummeling him on his arms as Archer protected his face from the man's blows. They slid across the table and sent trays of gray cubes flying.

With Green Teeth attempting to unscrew Archer's head from his body, Archer managed to jerk his knee up hard and fast into Green Teeth's unprotected groin. A guard, who seemed in no particular hurry to stop the fighting, finally activated his wrist-com. "Central," he said excitedly, "I have a disturbance in Population. Go to lockdown—"

Walton heard the message and smirked. "Hold that lockdown," he responded, and strode happily toward the conflict.

Green Teeth squealed, grabbed his testicles, and, with his free arm, hurled Archer across the room. Archer staggered to his feet to find the inmates staring at him, unimpressed. They might as well have called him a pussy. One inmate looked particularly contemptuous, and Archer realized, a second later, he was looking at the face of Pollux Troy. Green Teeth was lurching toward him, a ferocious towering bear, when Archer realized his own advantage was his agility. He leapt to the side as Green Teeth lunged, and, before he could recover, threw his body hard against the giant's massive head, using his shoulder to smash it into the steel of the wall.

Archer was winning the crowd over. Green Teeth growled and turned to his adversary, who sneered and swelled with fearlessness. Green Teeth's ramrod of a fist shot out, but Archer was ready. He sidestepped the punch, grabbed the extended arm, and yanked all 350 pounds of the enraged grizzly off-balance. The giant's crotch was completely unprotected when Archer's steel-covered toes jerked hard and straight into Green Teeth's testicles.

"Never—in—the—face," Archer said, accentuating each word with powerful kicks to the scrotum. Green Teeth bent over in agony. Archer's metal-bound foot was aching, so he switched to his fist for a devastating blow up the giant's chin and across his nose. The blow sent the giant reeling to the floor, bleeding profusely from his battered nose. Archer savored his triumph as Green Teeth eyed him hatefully through his tousled hair. As a matter of honor, he staggered to his feet for one more challenge.

Red Walton, who had done nothing so far to stop the fight, was no longer amused. "Lock 'em down," he said, matter-of-factly. Archer felt the mild shock again and realized his boots were gripped by the magnetic floor. Green Teeth flailed his arms hopelessly as blood from his nose ran down the black-and-white stripes of his jumpsuit. Archer gasped in agony when he felt Walton's shock stick in his spine, the pain exploding in an instant through every nerve of his body. He was bent backward when Walton thrust his fist into Archer's open diaphragm.

"Why me?" Archer gasped. "He started it." Walton answered by smashing him harder on the chin. Archer collapsed, but his feet were anchored to the floor, and his ankles twisted in agonizing pain as he fell.

"When I get out of here—" Archer rasped.

"You'll what?" Walton sneered.

"I'm going to have you fired."

Walton said nothing and looked at Archer with curiosity. Then Walton started laughing, a rich, belly laugh that ignited a chain reaction among the guards first and then the inmates. Archer looked around the room of convulsing men who had suddenly warmed to him. They wouldn't fuck with him either. Grateful for the humor, Walton turned all of his hostility on Green Teeth, whose real name was Dubov.

"Three strikes, and you're jerky, Dubov." The prisoner's eyes bulged in horror. *What's jerky?* Archer asked himself, as a cluster of guards converged on a screaming Dubov with shock sticks. He was suddenly silent since the sticks were set on stun. The guards took hold of his limbs and dragged him away as Walton addressed the other inmates.

"The rest of you get back to your suites," he shouted, "or no lunch tomorrow." The inmates groaned and shook their heads. They had heard him refer to their cells as suites over a thousand times. Archer struggled to stand as Walton stepped past him, and said, "Got a honeymoon suite for you, Archer. Champagne in a bucket, heart-shaped bed, Jacuzzi in the bathroom." Archer was scowling as he joined the line of cons. Pollux slowed to speak with him.

"Hey, bro . . ." Archer said, fighting every urge to knit his brow. Pollux stared at Archer, his eyes dissecting him.

"Bro? *Bro?*" Pollux spit out. "You're not my brother."

Chapter 7

Archer held his breath. After a moment, Pollux grinned. "The brother I know would never have been caught by that needle-dick Sean Archer," Pollux complained."At least tell me the bomb is still going off."

Archer exhaled. "They haven't found it yet. Listen, Pollux—" Though it repulsed him, Archer put an arm over Pollux's shoulder. Walton stared at them, threatening them with the shock stick until they were silent.

Archer crawled up a ladder to his tiny, steel-framed cell. Once all the prisoners were inside, all twenty-five hundred doors closed in unison. An older inmate, known as the Ancient One for his snowy beard, was locked out when he failed to reach his cell, which was stacked near the top. His frail, old voice screamed "No, no!"

as he was dragged away for some mysterious punishment.

The cell wasn't tall enough to stand in. Erewhon had no radio or television sets, no library, no laundry or license plate–making facilities. Archer guessed the prison was deep below the earth since he had experienced the compression discomfort he'd felt when he was in Tartarus. He looked at the steel bed which also served as sitting furniture. He vowed to appreciate the comfort of a sheet-fitted king-size mattress all the rest of his life.

"Castor," came a voice from the cell next to him. "This is for you." A trembling hand from the cell held out a baby-food jar of Scotch. Later, Archer would receive jars of bourbon and gin, several precious cigarettes, and the hard white food cubes which were used as currency. The inmates had strong reason to believe he was the new kingpin of Erewhon, and they were anxious to court his favor.

Castor was coming back from the black. It started first with pain—with aching, throbbing, unbearable stinging all over his head. Something soft and squishy was resting on his face, which felt strangely lighter. His eyes were wide-open, and when he shifted them, he could see the running spikes of the monitors. A puff of mist fell over his eyes, which were itching like a flea-infested dog. He tried blinking and couldn't. Why couldn't he blink? Was he paralyzed? No . . . he could work his fingers and clench his fist. He reached for his eyes to rub them and ripped off the mask. When he felt his eyes, he realized he had no lids, then realized he had no nose, ears, or mouth . . . all he felt were the rawly exposed muscles and bones of his face.

Reflexively, he jumped from the bed and tore the tubes and wires that tethered him to the machines. A wave of weakness passed through him, and he collapsed to the floor, groaning in agony. He struggled to stand and fumbled for an electric switch on the wall. The bulbs flickered on, and he stumbled to the bathroom, where he saw a mirror over the sink. Slowly he walked to the mirror. What he saw made him scream—a face like a muscle diagram in a medical text, with a gaping, lipless mouth and teeth gaping in abject horror.

He couldn't breathe. He would have vomited if there had been food in his stomach. Shaking uncontrollably, he was dry-heaving. When he had finally calmed down, he looked around the complex and found a desk covered with family pictures. One of them was of a middle-aged doctor with a long braid of hair kissing his wife on a beach in Bali.

After wrapping his head in gauze, Castor found the elevator and emerged into the darkened barn. He stepped out and realized he was on a cattle ranch overlooking the ocean. The sky was clear, a midnight blue, and spattered with the whorls of a billion stars. *It was a night that might have inspired van Gogh to paint, Castor thought. Or to cut off his ear.*

Through the chirping crickets and rumination of the cows, Castor heard muffled laughter and conversation. He crouched behind an oak tree and looked through the kitchen window of the ranch house. He saw the man with the silver braid and his wife in their housecoats, drinking milk and eating pie. His eyes followed their driveway to the mailbox. Walsh was their name. And they lived on 1216 Ramsey Canyon Drive. Lars and Lunt could use their *Thomas Guide* to find him. All Castor needed to do was call. Looking down on the Pacific Coast Highway, he eyed an open gas station and saw a public phone.

To get cigarettes, Castor tried sympathy on the clerk. When that didn't work, he unrolled the gauze. The clerk screamed and fell behind the counter. He pushed a carton of Marlboros at Castor and a handful of change. "Just leave!" he said, and Castor obliged him.

Lars or Lunt didn't believe it was him—he was supposed to be dead. And the sound of his voice was strange since he couldn't fully articulate without lips. They didn't believe a word of what he told them was true, but were intrigued enough to find out. For one thing, the person claiming to be Castor Troy was almost begging them. "I need you guys," he had said. "This is something I can't do alone."

An hour later, the Walshes were in bed when they were awakened by the screeching tires of a Range Rover. Within seconds, their front door had been knocked down. It sounded like a small army as the Swedes charged up the steps and kicked open the bedroom door. Selena Walsh clapped on the table lamp and shook when she saw the men aiming automatic weapons at her and her husband. Malcolm Walsh put on his glasses.

"Who are you people? What do you want?" he asked.

Castor elbowed his way through the beefy gates of Lunt and Lars. "I want my face," Castor said, using his teeth to bite down on a cigarette in order to puff it. The smoke drifted from cavities set in raw muscle, cartilage, and bone. Selena screamed, the first in a series of screams that night. *Hmmm,* Castor thought. *'A Starry Night.' Maybe I'll start with her ear first.*

Minutes later, Castor was holding a scalpel next to Selena's ear. He was threatening to go further when Walsh promised his complete cooperation. The first thing he did was give the Swedes access to the computer, where they reviewed the procedure. They called Castor over. He saw just what it was that stylish FBI agents were wearing on their skulls this season.

The prisoners were given forty-nine minutes a day for exercise. It was the time that most of them chose to smoke the daily allotment of one cigarette which was spiked with the same tranquilizing drug in the food. "The yard" was hardly like a yard at all. It was one more hall made of cold blue steel with a small skylight in the roof. Molded on opposite ends of the walls were basketball hoops. On another wall was a huge video screen with an image of Lake Ontario, its gentle waves lapping on a shore of pines.

"Castor Troy" was immediately drafted by both basketball teams since word of his abilities had quickly spread. Minutes into the game, he was jeered by the spectators. The first ball passed to him smacked him in the face. The second time he had the ball in his hands he attempted a jump shot from midcourt. The resulting air ball was picked off, passed all the way to the opposing side's basket, and sunk. His teammates, impressed by the way he had handled Dubov, hesitated to force him out of the game and risk his wrath. But Archer took a hint and joined Pollux on one of the few metal benches molded into the wall.

Pollux stared blankly at the image of Lake Ontario as he scratched his nose, his elbows, his tongue. He lit his cigarette and exhaled first through his nostrils, then his mouth, blowing the smoke to the left and right. He took another drag and spoke, smoke floating off of each word. "You realize, of course, this magnetic humming is designed to drive us insane. If we all don't get brain tumors first." Archer felt a mix of fascination and repulsion for Pollux as he watched him, a quirky, jerky man whose own body seemed to be fighting itself. Pollux turned his head in the direction of the nature scene.

"And that same cloying tape—over and over. It's like they're begging us to riot." Pollux looked around at their bleak surroundings. "Just where the fuck are we?" he asked.

Archer shrugged, as Pollux passed the butt. Uh-oh . . . it had burned to nearly halfway down and promised to be particularly noxious. Archer went to take a drag when he realized

Pollux was studying him. The smoke was in his mouth, and he hesitated to suck it down. When he did, he choked. Pollux's frantic, monkeylike behavior came to a standstill. He spoke in a slow, near whisper as his eyes slitted.

"I've been watching you."

Archer hardened, stared at Pollux. "Yeah, so?"

Pollux was flitting like a hummingbird again, his voice filled with an irritating melody. "Your jump shot has no arc. You used to swagger. Now you swish. You're gumming that butt like a Catholic-school girl." Pollux's eyes fell to Archer's hands.

"And why do you keep scraping at your finger?"

Pollux had noticed that Archer was reflexively tugging at his phantom wedding ring. Archer looked down at his ring finger and saw that Walsh had obscured the white band of skin with an artificial tanner. He shrugged and scratched one more time, as if he had finally taken care of an itch. Pollux's eyes were shifting as he dropped back into a slow, snaky hiss of a voice.

"I'm having doubts that you're . . . you."

Archer was still as a stone as Pollux reached for his face. He pulled down the left eye sack to expose Archer's globe, like a vet examining a sick basset hound. Archer clamped his hand on Pollux's face and pushed him hard. Pollux fell off the seat, leapt up, and jerked back his fist as if he might coldcock Archer. Pollux was making his ugliest face, his eyeballs full and white, daring his "brother" to push him again.

Archer considered the possible ways to meet this behavior, and finally settled on laughing. Pollux loosened as he heard a strange snigger from Archer that was developing into a guffaw. Archer put an arm around Pollux, who flinched at first, and then gave in. "You're as paranoid as ever," Archer managed between laughs. "Man, you gotta get back on your medication."

"And what exactly was my medication, big brother?"

Archer shrugged—a piece of cake. "Vivex. And Placanol. Depren-B. Assorted chill pills to level out those nasty highs and lows." Archer saw that a drag remained on the cigarette. He brought it smoothly to his lips and sucked back a rich and opaque cloud of smoke into his lungs. He held it for a moment, pretending to savor its poisons, then exhaled it directly in Pollux's face.

"Pollux, I was in a coma. My reflexes, my senses, my memory . . . everything's a fucking jumble. I can't even tell you why Dubov jumped me yesterday." Archer relaxed when he saw that Pollux's suspicion level had plummeted.

"How could you forget that?" Pollux

squawked. "You pollinated his wife the same day he was sent here."

"I did?"

"Yes!"

"Was she hot?"

"She was hotter before you passed her over to me."

"I've forgotten plenty. So I'm gonna need you to help me fill in the blanks."

Pollux's suspicion level was rising again. Archer came closer, whispered hard into Pollux's face. "Look around, bro. We've fucked over half the freaks in this dump. What's gonna happen to me if they think I've lost my mind? What's gonna happen to you?"

Pollux contemplated the other inmates. They were watching the Troy brothers out of the corners of their eyes, sizing them up like hungry sharks. Pollux looked at the Sudnick cousins, who were staring at them openly. The cousins had had a vendetta against the Troys since the day they had diverted a massive shipment of weapons away from the Chechen rebels and into the hands of the Russians. To their right, Annunzio Suarez and his lieutenants were watching, anxious to avenge the moment when the Troy brothers had hijacked their truck loaded with eight million dollars in crystal methedrine. Giving them a sideways glare were the Chang Gang, with whom the Troys had once drunk blood, and then shortly proceeded to relieve of some illicit military software. Pollux was searching for other enemies when Archer hugged him. Pollux pulled away, as usual, but Archer insisted.

"Hug me, bro. Show 'em we got nothing but love for each other."

Pollux fulfilled the next part of the ritual, and gave in to the bear hug. When Archer broke away, he yanked open his shirt exposing the tattoo of the Pyramids of Giza.

"I know I got this on my tenth birthday, but I can't remember why."

Archer tried to breathe regularly as he waited to see if Pollux would fall into the trap. His brow folded again, giving him the suspicious-cobra look.

"Come on!" he said, almost singing. "That was the worst day of our lives!"

Archer feigned a struggle with his memory. Knowing that he needed to look hurt, he thought of Mikey—and then felt awful for abusing his son's memory.

"Oh, Christ—Dad overdosed at County General," Archer said.

Pollux started bobbing his head frantically. "Retching and convulsing while those bastards didn't even try to save his sorry ass. You gave him mouth-to-mouth! Man, even then you had some constitution."

Archer was jerked out of his persona for a moment, to ponder this unexpected side of Castor Troy. Pollux got misty, and said, "Remember what you swore to me at the funeral?"

"Uh . . . to kill the doctors?" Archer vamped.

"After that," said Pollux, getting childlike. His hands were clasped, and his face looked almost sweet when, coyly, he turned away and lightly ran a finger down Archer's shoulder. "You pwomised . . . you'd always take care of me."

Pwomised, Archer thought to himself. Of all the disgusting things he had witnessed in the last week, this sickened him the most. This would be his shining moment if he could manage not to be violently ill. He cleared his throat. "And I bet I've kept that pwomise," he said, somehow looking into Pollux's eyes.

"Only one you've never broken."

Pollux continued to stare at him with large, luminous eyes that were coating "Castor" in affection. Archer's smile crumbled, his timing somewhat off, as he suddenly reverted to his real agenda: find the bomb.

"Fuck the past," he spit out. "We've got the future to look forward to." Archer pulled the jars of booze from the loosened hem of his shirt and slyly passed the Scotch to Pollux. "We still have Saturday night," Archer said, and smirked.

"No shit," said Pollux, downing the liquid. Archer slipped him another cigarette, watched him get pensive. "Ten million bucks," Pollux sighed. "Now the Cali drug lords get to keep it."

Cali drug lords? Archer was shamed. No one at the Bureau had a clue about this. He used his genuine dismay to drench his next lines.

"That's not the worst part, Pollux."

Pollux squinted. "What could be worse than losing ten million bucks?"

"Being stuck in this shithole when it blows. What you built was a work of art. It belongs in the Smithsonian." Archer successfully managed to stare at Pollux as if *he* were a work of art. Pollux beamed and drew on his smoke. "Yeah," he said, as smoke escaped with every word, "the L.A. Convention Center will have to do."

Archer nodded. Then he smiled. "Thanks, Pollux" he said.

Pollux was startled. "Thanks?" he repeated. He was suddenly disoriented, looking straight at Archer and strongly sensing some other mystery where there ought not to be any. Archer realized he had dropped his facade and was reveling in his triumph. His enthusiasm about something was now quite obvious, but its sudden appearance was alarming to Pollux, and its source incomprehensible. Archer was thinking to himself that everything he had been through was worth it. In the back of his mind, he was even thinking about the book he would write, and how much he would get when they sold his story to Hollywood. With the money he could send Jamie to college and take Eve on a grand tour of Europe.

"I guess they really did fuck you up," Pollux said, squinting at his brother. Giddy and uncaring about what Pollux might have sensed, Archer took a ladylike sip of his booze. Pollux was instantly horrified, staring at Archer's face, then at the full jar. Archer realized his mistake—sipping was wrong. He downed the jar, but it was too late. Suddenly ill at ease, Pollux frantically scratched his neck, his ears, and his armpits. At that very moment, the image on the wall screen broke up and was replaced by the six-foot-high image of Red Walton.

"Your attention, inmates. Recently, one of your number violated the three-strikes rule. Caspar Dubov, inmate number fourteen fifty-six, has been reconsigned to the Desiccation Ward for the remainder of his life sentence."

Pollux, Archer, and the rest of the inmates were deadly quiet as Walton continued. The video camera showed him in the vicinity of a large, glass-lidded pod. Inside, Dubov was constrained by steel bands. He was screaming for mercy in a raspy yet suddenly childlike voice. "NO! NO! PLEASE! I PROMISE I'LL BE GOOD!" Archer wasn't sure what was going to happen to him, but he was overwhelmed with pity.

Walton pressed a series of buttons and spoke into his wrist-com. "Activate desiccation pod number one twenty-three," he said, then winked into the camera, which shifted its focus to the pod.

A series of tubes that ended in flowers of thin hypodermic needles were pushed into Dubov's sides. Dubov's screams were muffled as the glass lid locked over the pod. Archer almost turned away as Dubov's screaming grew louder still. In a receptacle above the pod, a bioengineer flipped on a machine, and yellow fluid collected in a receptacle. Dubov could scream no longer. In a matter of seconds, he was turned into a dried-out broomstick of a man. His eyes shut in abject misery. Suddenly, the pod was inverted. A hydraulic lift was returning the pod to its slot in the ceiling. The video cameraman got under the pod as it rose, and Dubov's skeletal face got smaller. In the wide shot of the ceiling, the inmates saw over a hundred desiccated prisoners, barely kept alive under a low orange light. The camera turned its lens back on Walton.

"Thank you for your attention, gentlemen. And remember. In the jerky ward, no one can hear you shrink."

Archer did push-ups in the narrow confines of his cell. He was bored and anxious, but had the itchy contentment of someone with a secret he would soon get to tell. He was turning his attention to sit-ups when Red Walton banged his shock stick between the bars. "Visitor," he said, and Archer smiled. He would never be so happy to see Ned Brodie's apelike mug and smell his overcoat reeking from mothballs. Miller would be there, and he would kiss her, whether she liked it or not. Hell, he was even going to kiss Brodie. They would stop at a bar on the way back and get drunk off their asses—well, they would get drunk once the bomb was dismantled. Walton spoke into his wrist-com, and Archer's bars swung open.

He was genuinely swaggering as he strolled in his lockdown boots to the interrogation room. Perhaps this was one aspect of Castor Troy he might integrate into his own personality. Once in the room, he felt the boots lock down. Archer was beaming as the guillotine door rushed open. His exhilaration disintegrated when he found himself staring into the blue eyes of the visitor.

Archer felt as if he had been electrocuted, but it hadn't killed him. He was looking at his own face on someone else's head. He kept staring, hoped he was dreaming, but realized he was more than awake.

"What's the matter? Don't you like the new me?" said his visitor, with Archer's own voice.

Archer stared at the image of his former self, trying to understand. He was captivated by the smirk on the face, the mocking twinkle in the eyes. He had a sudden, terrifying realization. "Castor?" Archer croaked out.

"Not anymore," replied Castor Troy, ghoulishly smiling with what had once been Sean Archer's lips.

Chapter 8

Archer's knees buckled. He would have fallen if the boots hadn't kept him in place. "It can't be. It's impossible," he gasped.

Castor sneered. "I believe the phrase Dr. Walsh used was 'titanically remote.' Who knows? Maybe the trauma of having my face cut off pulled me out. Or maybe Satan is finally running the show. Have something for you. I know you don't get the papers in here."

Castor threw the *Los Angeles Times* on the floor. Archer read the headline as it unfurled. "TEN DEAD IN INFERNO." Next to the story was a picture of Malcolm and Selena Walsh.

"Terrible tragedy," Castor said. "Walsh was such a genius, but so selfish with his artistry. I actually had to *torture* his wife to convince him to perform the same surgery on me."

Archer was sickened. "You killed them?"

"Of course I killed them, you *dumb fuck*. And torched every shred of evidence that proves who you really are." Castor lit another Gitane, and said, "Swallow this one, baby. You are going to be in here the rest of your life."

Archer felt a constriction in his throat and lungs. His head was pounding. He realized he wanted to cry . . . before his worst enemy. "What are you going to do, Castor?"

Castor's eyes slitted as he pointed his finger at Archer. "Let's get something straight. I'm Archer. You're Castor."

"What are you going to do?" Archer shouted. His face was purple with rage. Castor chuckled, and casually drew on his smoke.

"You've given me a freedom I haven't had in years, and the power to make it pay off in ways I never thought possible. But this is America, isn't it? One day, a pauper, the next, a prince. And I owe it all to you."

Castor threw the smoking butt between Archer's boots. "Now, if you'll excuse me, I've got an important government job to abuse and a beautiful wife to fuck. Excuse me . . . I mean 'make love to.' Have a nice day."

Archer felt like an oil gusher that had been ignited into an all-consuming inferno. He yanked futilely at his boots, his arms lunging as

Castor strolled to the door. "Come back here, you piece of shit!" Archer screamed.

"Sean, this is so unbecoming of you," Castor said, summoning Walton with a plunge button near the door. Walton rushed in to see Archer's arms flailing. Walton quickly set the shock stick to stun and zapped Archer. He instantly dropped to the floor with a sickening clunk as his chin crashed against the steel.

"Sorry, sir," said Walton.

"It's quite all right, Red. You never know what to expect from a psychopathic criminal." Castor pivoted on his heel.

Sean realized blood was dribbling down his chin as he came to. The guards were dragging him back to his cell. Walton was almost yanking Archer's arm from its socket.

"Better be nice, Castor. You could get mighty lonely in here now that Pollux is gone."

"Pollux is—what?" Archer mumbled as he was heaved up to his cell and shoved in.

"Sean Archer cut him a deal for turning state's evidence. He's been released."

The bars closed on the cell. Archer clutched at them as Walton marched off. "Walton, you have to listen to me—right now."

Walton turned and gave Archer one of his

lipless grins. "Or what, Castor? You'll have me fired? You're confined until I say otherwise." When Archer continued his protests, Walton mumbled a command into his wrist-com. Instantly, a panel of steel rolled over the cell's bars and eliminated all light and sound. Archer collapsed in the darkness, having never felt more alone. He rubbed his face and was repulsed—he remembered it wasn't his face at all.

Tito's housemate, Anson, was shopping at Gelson's. Their friends Miguel and Brian had returned from Romania with their newly adopted daughter and were bringing her over for dinner. Anson was attempting to cook the girl's national dishes and realized he needed barley and fresh beets for something called *pistou*. Tito's job was to buy beer, a Romanian phrase book, and tack up a poster of Nadia Comaneci. Outside the house, he stopped to pick up the newspaper from the doorstep.

Castor had been circling the block earlier, driving in Archer's car with Archer's wallet and computer address book tucked in his pockets. Tito was shocked to enter the kitchen of his restored Spanish duplex to find someone seated at the table drinking mescal from the bottle. Tito dropped his sack, whipped out his pistol, then recovered with a nervous laugh when he saw it was "Sean Archer."

"Jesus Christ, Sean. You just gave me the shock of my life. What the hell happened?"

"You're the secret agent," Castor said. "You tell me." Castor, his legs up on the table, took a swig of liquor and set the bait. Would Tito take it?

Tito lowered his gun and gave Castor a scolding look. "Christ. You're in a mood," Tito said, picking up the sack. "What happened? Pollux wasn't fooled for a minute, and you had to pull out, right?"

Castor smiled, as Tito dug through his pockets. "Don't go home without this," Tito said, producing Archer's wedding band and setting it on the table.

Castor eyed it with disdain, then forced it over his slightly thicker finger. The ring gouged the pad above his knuckle. Noticing the struggle with the ring, Tito felt strangely insecure—something wasn't right.

"Thanks," Castor said. "Didn't feel like myself without it. How about a beer for me?"

"First mescal. Now a beer." Tito emptied the bag and picked up the newspaper. He made out the headline about Walsh's death and went stiff. He was starting to breathe heavily and realized he had to unfreeze. He shifted awkwardly to the fridge. "Beer coming up," he said, pulling one from the carton. In a sudden move, he turned and tossed the bottle at Castor. Castor raised his right hand, fumbled awkwardly, and dropped the bottle on the floor. The cap loosened, and foam sprayed in a thin jet as Tito went for his gun.

Castor was too fast. His left hand had already been holding his pistol down at his side, and he was firing before Tito could take aim. The first bullet went through Tito's throat. His mouth gushed with red bubbles as his trembling hand dropped the gun. Castor looked at the fizzing bottle. "I'll have to work on that," he said. The second bullet caught Tito between the eyes.

Castor took the beer with him. He wasn't surprised that a responsible type like Sean Archer had a *Thomas Guide* in his car, and he soon found Archer's bit of suburban bliss. The Olds cruised smoothly through the lanes of manicured lawns. Kids were playing tag, women were borrowing sugar, men were weeding their dichondra and snipping at oleanders. "Christ, what a life," Castor said as his neck stretched to catch a street address. "I may never get a hard on again."

Dressed for work, Eve watched blandly as the Oldsmobile passed the house. She was mildly biting her lip when she watched the car back up and park. Castor shoved the beer under the seat, jumped out, and smiled broadly. Eve liked it when he smiled, which he rarely did, but at the moment, it was impossible for her to return it.

"I suppose it was only a matter of time before you forgot where we lived," she said.

"Sorry. Work was just murder today."

Castor couldn't stop grinning. She was much sexier than he expected. She walked to her car, and he waited to follow her so he could check out her caboose. Nice . . . a small waist leading to a plump, heart-shaped little rump. She put on her sunglasses, turning away from him.

"I didn't expect you back so soon. What happened to your important assignment?"

"What do you know about it?" he asked. Shit—would he have to kill her, too?

"What do *I* know about it? As much as ever, Sean. Nothing."

Castor was grinning like a bastard again. "It didn't work out the way everyone thought it would. Where are you off to?"

She shrugged. "I've got surgery." Castor mustered a concerned look.

"Surgery? Are you okay?"

She lowered her sunglasses and rolled her eyes. Castor spotted her medical bag. *Oops.*

"Don't try to charm me. I'm still angry." She kept walking to her Volvo. "There's leftovers in the fridge. A pizza, I think. And some bad Thai."

"Have fun at work," Castor said. Eve threw her bags in the car, silent as she plopped into the seat.

"Baby, wait a minute," he pleaded, feigning hurt.

"What?" she snapped, starting the car. Castor stepped to the window, placed his hand around her neck, and kissed her mouth. She gawked at him. "What is with you?" she asked.

"Don't I usually kiss my wife good-bye?"

"No!"

Eve pulled out. Castor watched her drive off and licked his lips. The bitch tasted good. He knew she'd be like all these gashes who work for a living: tell her she's beautiful and give her some jewelry and she'd melt like butter. As Eve drove away, she imagined she had tasted cigarettes and Budweiser on her husband's mouth.

Castor took a good look at Archer's house, a fully restored two-story bungalow. "What a dump," he muttered. The house was so fucking *old.* He entered the living room and looked around at the dark, wooden furniture from the turn of the century. The Tiffany lamps and Parrish prints were selected to reflect the

Nouveau aesthetic. Castor found it odd, mystifying, and ugly.

He found what he recognized immediately as Archer's office with its old sports trophies, FBI manuals, and collection of Tom Clancy novels. He sat at the desk and worked his way through the drawers. *Who is this little kid whose picture is everywhere? Must be the boy I killed.* Castor sorted through old Christmas cards, bank statements (FBI agents made shitty money), and finally found a scrapbook of Archer's adventures. Inside were pictures and newspaper articles about Archer and his people. Castor could match the names of the address book to faces now. Here were Wanda Tan, Buzz Williams, Loomis, and Victor Lazarro.

Craving a cigarette, Castor closed the drawers to hunt for tobacco. He figured the kitchen was the best place to start and searched through the drawers of the sunny breakfast nook. Eve had set a crystal vase of freshly cut dahlias on the table. His despair grew as he searched the final drawer. This one was full of candles and cookie cutters. In the back he saw several small notebooks. The one on top was covered with a Japanese *ukeyoe* print of white-faced women smoking clay pipes. Inside the book was off-white paper flecked with dried flower petals. It was faintly scented with sandalwood and filled with precise, delicate writing, the kind of script one would expect from a lady surgeon.

The first page had a printed warning: *This diary is the property of Eve Donovan Archer. It would be a violation of our love and trust should my husband, daughter, or friends find this book and read my most private thoughts. Please return this book to its proper place before reading any further.*

Castor flipped through the pages and saw that the last entry was from just a few days ago.

> Sean missed Date Night again. Felt like an idiot for driving to Jurgenson's to buy angelica at 19 dollars a quarter pound just to make him a Nesselrode pie. I really have to stop blaming him for the disappointment I feel. If I know he's bound to flake, then I'm the one responsible for having the expectation. Oh well . . . I just imagined that a romantic dinner and the revelation of a lacy, peach-colored bra and matching lace panties might end the dry spell. It's close to two months now since we've made love. . . ."

Castor smirked. "What a fucking loser," he muttered to himself.

The phone rang. Castor almost jumped . . . it was his phone now, he should pick it up. But where was it? He heard a door creak open and shoved Eve's diary back in the drawer. From the kitchen he could make out the perfect cream cheese of a teenage girl's legs as she raced down the stairs to pick up the cordless. He stood to the side of the kitchen wall and watched Jamie giggling as she talked on the phone. She wore nothing but panties and a cropped T-shirt. He turned on the kitchen light, and Jamie turned to look at him. When she saw it was her father, she wrinkled her nose and turned her back. *The plot thickens,* Castor thought. Archer's wife had a great rump, but his daughter's little hams were high-and-mighty. When Jamie realized her "father" was still watching her, she took the cordless into her own room, slammed the door, and lit a Marlboro.

When Castor smelled the tobacco burning, his lungs ached with smoke hunger, and he took the stairs two at a time. He pressed his ear to the door.

"My father's home," he could hear her say. "I haaaaaate him . . . yes, I got your e-mails . . . the poem was *to*tally sweet. Did you make that up? Really?"

Castor knocked at the door.

"Hang on a sec," she said softly, then covered the mouthpiece. "WHAT?" she shouted at the door. She saw it was opening, ran over, and tried to slam it shut, but Castor thrust his foot inside.

"Karl, I'll call you back," she said, and pressed the OFF button. She leaned against the door. "You're not respecting my boundaries, father figure."

"Don't speak to me like that . . . young lady," Castor essayed, his idea of father-speak. "C'mon Janie. Let me in."

Castor pushed hard and barged menacingly into the room. He saw the girl looking at him in curious contempt. "*Janie?*" she repeated, with one side of her face pulled up. What Castor did next, she seemed to be completely thrown by. He eyed her up and down before settling on her face with what looked like a seductive gaze. Over her shoulder, Castor eyed an embroidered pillow with her name on it. She felt scared and tiny.

"I don't think you heard me . . . Jamie. You have something I want."

The girl was frozen, battling different feelings about her "father's" strange behavior. At the moment he had the sinister charms of a predator—she was feeling the insidious flattery of being preyed upon. If he tried to touch her, what would she do? Castor's arm snaked toward her . . . it seemed to be in slow motion . . . and then it went past her. He picked up the pack of Marlboros and shook one out.

"Ummm . . . Penny left those here," she said.

Castor shrugged, tilted his head in a charming fashion, and lit up. His eyes blinked slowly as he French-inhaled, then released the smoke in a long, steady stream.

"I won't tell Mom if you don't," he said.

She stared at him, barely able to get out her words. "When did you start smoking?"

She looked at the way he stood. His legs were crossed and one hand was fisted and pressed low to his hip, which thrust provocatively in an angle below his chest. He grinned freely as he shook out some more smokes and slipped them into his shirt pocket. "You'll be seeing a lot of changes around here. Pappa's got a brand new bag."

Castor pivoted and swaggered away. Jamie stared. "*Pappa?*" she whispered, and gingerly sat on her bed.

He wasn't sure what time Archer showed up for work in the morning, but he thought nine o'clock was a safe bet. *Walk like white bread,* he told himself as he entered the lobby checkpoint and donned his stern "Archer" face. He nodded a good morning to the fat guard, who was eating a sandwich. Castor heard the guard's gravelly voice behind him. "Mr. Archer, you didn't check in." Check in? Archer turned to see another agent press his thumb to the ID pad. "Sorry . . . Edward," Castor said, looking at the man's name tag.

"Edward?" said the man, smiling to reveal a cave of hideously irregular teeth spackled in the spaces with Wonder bread and salmon salad. "Since when did we get so formal?"

"Sorry . . . Eddie," Archer said, pressing his thumb to the ID pad. His cool was cooked for a second—did Walsh give him the right prints? The monitor hesitated before it turned from red to green, and he was waved in. He recognized Wanda Tan and gave her a formal good morning.

"Good morning to you," she responded, slightly surprised. Archer usually grunted "hello" in the mornings before ducking into his office.

"Where is Pollux Troy?" he asked.

"The interrogation room. With Lazarro."

Castor took a right when he heard Wanda's voice.

"The interrogation room, Sean."

"Right," said Castor, spinning in the other direction. He had been here for questioning once before—was this the way? The hall seemed to go on forever past endless offices. Castor finally found a door mercifully painted with the word "*interrogation.*" Outside the first chamber, Lazarro stood with hands clasped behind his back, watching Pollux and his interrogator through a two-way mirror. Pollux had an omelet before him, with cheese gushing out and home fries on the side. He struggled to eat it with his hands bound by cuffs. Castor took a second to recognize the man outside the booth as Lazarro.

"How's our star witness, Victor?" Castor asked.

"Hasn't told us a damn thing except that he wants catsup with his potatoes." Lazarro's fingers twiddled nervously behind him. "Assuming that bomb is out there, we're almost out of time. Jesus Christ, Sean! We're talking about a catastrophe!"

"Just leave me alone with him for five minutes, Victor. Trust me. He'll crack."

Lazarro turned a stony face to Castor and rocked angrily on the balls of his feet. "I know you have an instinct about this, Sean. But you cutting a deal with this particular psychopath . . ." Lazarro walked off, then turned to him. "I don't like it, Sean. I don't like it at all."

When he was gone, Castor entered the booth. He jerked the blinds down and yanked the mikes from their hookups.

"Pollux, you're supposed to be snitching. Making me look good."

"Look good? Seeing that face makes me want to puke." Pollux pushed his food away. Castor picked up the plate and worked on the omelet.

"*You* want to puke? I'm the one who has to look at this butt-ugly mug every time I pass a mirror. Look at my eyes, my chin, my perfect nose—gone. They might as well have stitched his ass to my head."

Looking in the two-way mirror, Castor reconsidered a face that by most standards was considerably more handsome than his original one. "That fucker took my life, so I'm taking his."

"What?" Pollux asked. His shoulders were nervously rolling, and he was scratching at the insides of his thighs.

"You heard me. I'm going straight, bro."

Pollux stared at his brother. "Did Archer take your brain, too?"

"Just imagine for a moment. Dillinger as J. Edgar Hoover. Carlos the Jackal running Interpol. Muammar Qaddafi heading the Mossad . . ."

Pollux listened intently. All his twitching stopped as his mind suddenly opened to the possibilities.

"I'll have the biggest private army in the world at my disposal," Castor continued. "And the best part is, I'm the *good* guy."

"No," said Pollux, with a double-wide grin. "The best part is since it's a government job, they can't fire you." Pollux's grin suddenly fell as he looked at his cuffed hands. "What about me, Castor?"

Castor stopped chewing and nodded solemnly. The plan was unfolding before him. "You're going to 'confess.' I'll be a hero, poised and ready for a big promotion." Castor lit a smoke and stuck it in Pollux's mouth. "And you, Pollux . . . you'll be a free man."

Had the Bureau found the bomb on their own, it would have been difficult but possible for them to disarm it. Castor had returned to the Convention Center by himself to further complicate the bomb's trappings, to add another layer of decoys that would confound the bomb squad. Once these were set in place, he visited Pollux again, announced that he had cracked, and joined the squad which had converged on the building in minutes.

When the porcelain case had been removed, the squad was stunned by circuitry and wiring of indecipherable logic. It resembled something that might have been found in the control panel of an alien spaceship. Numerous components glowed evilly when the team leader realized the circuits were full of decoys to deflect attention from the active circuits. What was genuinely presented by the bomb maker for the squad's benefit was a highly advanced yet completely recognizable vibration detector. The squad captain felt weak and loose in his bowels as he realized they now had less than four minutes. The technician blanched—both were out of their league. Castor waited impatiently outside and removed his blast visor.

"Jesus Christ," whispered the squad leader. "Any suggestions?"

"Yeah. Run," answered the technician as his back tensed and he felt a drip of sweat from under his armpit race down his trunk. Castor reentered, looking grim.

"It's protected by a vibration detector, sir. One snip of the wires and . . ." The captain couldn't finish his sentence.

"Evacuate your team, Captain," said Castor, as coolly as possible.

"Sir, you can't disarm it," the technician protested.

"Just go!" Castor shouted. The squad was relieved to follow his command, and they scurried like hares. Making sure he was alone, Castor pulled a modified cellular phone from his pocket. With a simple rewiring, it was now a radio controller. He pressed the pound sign and the bomb's glow rapidly faded. He looked at the timer, which showed twenty-six seconds remaining until detonation.

I don't know about that, he said to himself, his finger pressed to his mouth as he considered his options. He pressed the star button on the phone and the bomb was activated again. Waiting until it got to four seconds, he shut it off. *That's better*, he thought. He took a small bottle of Evian and splashed his face and collar before reemerging with the trophy of the triggers, twin canisters whose A and B fluids would never meet. He rewired the phone and called Lazarro.

"I did it," Castor said. In a few minutes, the press and camera crews would be converging on him. Castor's one thought was that a particular someone should see exactly what had been achieved that day.

Miserable to the core, Archer paced around the edges of the basketball game. "Yard" was the one time they were actually allowed to walk. The scenery on the vidscreen was always the same, the same tape of Lake Ontario. But it was easier on the eye than the swarm of inmate faces that flowed and eddied around Archer, a rat-faced, fish-faced, monkey-faced series of eyesores. He was careful to keep up his reserve, to flare his shoulders defiantly and assert his right to walk where he pleased. So far no one stood in his way, but several inmates sensed that without Pollux, "Castor" would weaken. They wouldn't have to send him gifts of cigarettes and booze or surrender their dessert cubes. He was trying to shake what he felt was madness buzzing in his head and picked up his pace, as if he could walk it out of his mind. The wall screen suddenly flashed, and a buzzer alerted the inmates. Were they shrinking someone else today? Red Walton's face filled the screen, and Archer nearly shuddered.

"A special privilege today, gentlemen: Television. By order of Agent Sean Archer of the Federal Bureau of Investigation."

The inmates jeered. Archer felt his heart pumping. The picture switched to a broadcast from Cable News Network.

A sweating Castor Troy looked exhausted yet stoic as he carried the disarmed bomb from out of the Convention Center. Over the image, an anchorman set the scene. "An FBI agent is being hailed as a hero. Agent Sean Archer disarmed a powerful bomb at the Los Angeles Convention Center just seconds before it was set to explode. Let's get the latest from Valerie Rice."

At first Castor played the role of reluctant

hero for the media, but he was soon basking in the flashing bulbs, the clamoring, the shouted questions. An attractive blond news reporter narrated in the foreground. The cons were not disgusted enough to refuse to celebrate the sudden vision of a woman, even if she was only an electronic image, and they hooted and wolf-whistled. Archer could hardly hear what she said.

"The bomb's apparent target was Eduardo Castillo, the chief justice of the Colombian Supreme Court. Castillo was due to make a surprise appearance here today," said Valerie, who turned to Castor and thrust the microphone in his face as he walked past. He was muttering about "getting back to work."

"Mr. Archer, do you have any idea who might have planted it?"

Archer watched Castor take in the woman's lovely features and stop to answer her question.

"That's classified," Castor answered. "But if he's listening, I have a message for him." Castor looked directly in the camera. "Nice try. Now you know who's really in charge." And then Castor raised his hand to his face . . . and stroked it.

Archer could not have imagined the level of rage he felt at that moment. Surely, no human in the history of the world had felt an anger and a hatred this intense, an inner inferno that would have made hell seem a cool and shady place. And then he realized that Castor Troy was wearing his clothes. Archer was sure he was going to combust. When he resumed breathing, his eyes fell on a guard using his thumbprint on the security scan-pad for a corridor off-limits to the cons. Archer felt the faintest hope as he looked at his own fingers and realized his prints were intact under the grafts Walsh had made. Was Erewhon's computer hooked up to the FBI mainframe in Washington? If it was, his prints might clear the scanner.

Archer remembered that nothing in the prison had a sharp surface. When he returned to his cell, he used the blunt point of his eyetooth to tear into the skin graft on his right thumb of Castor's plain whorls. Archer peeled away the sharply stinging skin and looked at his thumb, red, raw, and throbbing. But underneath, Archer could make out his own ulnar loops.

The fat security guard beamed at Castor when he returned to the office. As he swaggered down the hall, he sensed their attention and smiled in anticipation of a hero's return. A few coworkers gave him a thumbs-up but stayed seated at their desks. They all knew not to applaud. Castor stopped suddenly at the coffee station and surveyed the blank faces.

"Don't you guys watch TV? Where's the parade? Get some booze in here and bring up some hookers from the holding tank." Everyone stared at Castor, a few in disgust, and everyone in surprise. He made the sudden realization that the booze and hookers suggestion was way out of line, then laughed as if it had been a joke. For some, it was the first time they had seen Archer smile, and they were charmed. A few women found him suddenly sexy. Loomis, the bold rookie, ventured forward, unabashedly grinning, and started to clap. He extended his hand, and Castor gave him a hearty handshake. Others started clapping, leading to rousing applause. Castor shook other hands and took short, modest bows. When the applause died, he addressed them.

"Loomis, Buzz, uh, Wanda . . . all of you, really. I want to say thanks from the bottom of my heart. Thank you all for enduring me all those years I was an insufferable boor. From now on, consider me reborn."

He looked around the room. They were flabbergasted. Loomis started a second round of applause, which was louder than the first. "Thank you, yes. You are all too kind," Castor said, backing into his office. Wanda and Kim Brewster were staring with the rest. "Stop the presses," Wanda said. "Sean Archer found a personality."

"Maybe he had one surgically implanted," Kim said, and realized she had files in her hand she needed to return to her boss's cabinet.

Castor was answering e-mail when she entered and opened a bottom drawer. He jumped up, slapped her rump, and said "Hiya, Kim." Stunned, she turned to look at him. "I'm gonna get some coffee," he said. "You need one?"

"No . . . no thank you," she stammered, and stood there blinking, as Castor sped away.

When he returned, Castor found Lazarro seated at his desk. He set dark, glowering eyes on Castor, who froze and returned the stare. Lazarro held up a yellow legal pad. "I see you're already practicing your executive signature," he said, tossing the pad on the desk. Castor shrugged. He had been practicing Archer's signature. "What's up, Victor?" Castor asked, casually leaning against the wall.

Lazarro's pitch rose, and his words were fast and clipped. "You know perfectly well 'what is up.' You went behind my back and sent all of your bomb memos to Washington. Do you know how that made me look?"

Castor shrugged, took a sip of coffee. "Like an idiot?" he deadpanned.

"Yes. Like an idiot!" Lazarro boomed. "An incompetent, aging, criminally negligent idiot!"

"Victor, I was just following procedure."

"Procedure? You sent them a memo in which I totally disputed the threat of a bomb."

"You did dispute it, didn't you?"

"So did you!"

Lazarro spun in the chair and looked out the window. "Christ, Sean. You knew they were looking for an excuse to put me out to pasture. How could you do this? We've been friends for fifteen years. I taught you everything you know."

Lazarro sighed and pretended to be watching a sanitation truck as men rolled a Dumpster to the tines of its front. Castor turned to the window as well. "So there's nothing else to say," Castor said, not meeting Lazarro's eyes.

Lazarro felt stabbed as he stood from the chair. Mustering his dignity, he stood, straightened his shoulders, and glared at the sudden stranger. "Don't think I'm going down without a fight," he snarled.

Castor turned to see if he had left, but Lazarro had planted his feet in the doorway, waiting for Castor's response. He barely restrained a snigger before returning to the window. Lazarro walked quickly away, sure that "Archer" was hiding something. Even if it meant they would both go down, Lazarro would find out what that was.

Castor turned to a bookshelf and picked up a family picture of the Archers. He rubber-faced as he exaggerated Sean's frozen photo smile. When he turned to a mirror to see if he was getting it right, Castor warmly grinned at himself. *Sean Archer—your career is finally taking off,* he thought. When he set the picture back in its place, his eye was drawn to a dusty text: *You and the FBI: A Primer for New Employees.* He closed the door and sat at the desk.

The book was tedious. Whenever Castor got bored with it, thoughts of sex intruded. Miss Brewster kept coming to mind. The tight minidress she was wearing was practically an invitation, but no . . . he was up for a promotion, and any kind of sexual-harassment shit would blow his chances. He read a few more pages, found himself feeling horny again, then realized something—he was a married man.

Chapter 9

Jamie was practicing free throws in the backyard when Castor returned with bags from the grocery store. She had dyed her hair black, was wearing pale purple lipstick, and drawn thick black lines, with spikes on the ends, around her eyes. It was a somewhat strange sight, as if Cleopatra were shooting hoops. She missed again when Castor asked, "How about a game of horse?"

Her eyes rolled up in her head, and her mouth cracked to emit a brief pant of disgust. "Don't ask me to beat your butt again, father figure. It's harmful to my developing psyche."

"Afraid you'll lose?" Castor asked, setting down the bags.

She bounced the ball low in his direction. He scooped it up and crisply sank a free throw. *Swish.* She glared at him, then tossed an air ball.

"H," Castor said, as he dribbled twice and buried another one. Jamie retrieved the ball and sneered at him. She readied to take a shot when he stopped her.

"Try putting a higher arc on the ball. And square your shoulders to the basket."

Her mouth and nose were wrinkled to an ugly button, but he could see she was listening. She pushed the ball up as he had, and sank the shot. Her face relaxed a moment, and, with the slightest of nods, she acknowledged she was pleased. Castor grinned and was returning to the bags when he heard the nasal honk of a '97 Beamer pulling into the driveway.

"Gotta go, Daddy. Karl's here."

Daddy! he thought. Castor was pleased she had not called him "father figure," then asked himself why he was pleased—she wasn't his kid. His moment of triumph was instantly eviscerated when he saw Karl. He was clean-cut, a preppie, and his polo shirt had a tiny insignia of a lamb being held aloft in a sling. The shirt was tucked into ironed khakis. When he turned to Castor to wave and smile, Karl revealed strong white teeth which had been perfected by orthodontics. Castor hated his auburn hair, which was short and shiny, and the oily way in which he dramatized the opening of the car door for Jamie. The boy's fastidious appearance didn't fool Castor for a moment. He sensed he had much in common with Karl. And Karl might get to Jamie before he could.

As she drove home with the sun nearly melted in the west, Eve was planning to watch *Jeopardy!* and eat a sandwich in bed. Sean's car was in the driveway, but the house was dark, and she figured he was already in bed. Tired and sleepy as she was, it was an effort for her to walk the five steps up to the door. It was pitch-black inside the house, and her hand fumbled for the light switch. She heard the deep, sensual scrape of a wooden match igniting. Her husband's face flickered in the soft orange light—he was still in his suit, wearing a tie that had lingered, unworn, in the closet for years. Castor lit candles, which illuminated a perfectly set table, and smiled warmly at her confusion.

"Don't tell me you forgot, Eve."

The blank look on her face said she had.

"It's Date Night!" Castor nearly sang, pouring her a glass of wine from a dark green bottle. He handed her the glass. As she drank, his warm gaze melted something dark and icy inside her. She shuddered in delight when he pulled her chair out and kissed the back of her neck when she was seated. Eve stuffed down her immediate suspicions because she wanted to enjoy it for a moment—but he had to be up to something. He looked at her adoringly before turning into the kitchen and returning with a carefully arranged salad of baby greens, thinly sliced walnuts, shredded smoked gouda, and a hazelnut vinaigrette. She tasted it and found it mild and delicious. Afterward, there was fresh corkscrew pasta with a tomato, cream, and shallot sauce.

"Why do I feel like I'm on a blind date?" she asked.

Castor grinned and gingerly dabbed at his mouth with his napkin. "It's important . . . to keep some mystery . . ." he said, gently dropping his words like rose petals. "So things stay . . . unpredictable."

Eve studied him as he raised his glass to her. Her smile faded as she gathered what was going on.

"Unpredictable, Sean? You? You're about as unpredictable as the tide." She dropped her fork and took a quick drink of wine, snapping the glass back to the table. "How long are you going to be gone *this* time?" she asked.

"Gone?" The perplexed look on his face was perfectly executed.

"Isn't that what this is all about? The wine, cooking me dinner—when's your next assignment, Sean?"

Castor reached for her other hand, which she was nervously tapping on the table. "I'm not going anywhere, Eve."

"You always say that. And then you leave."

Castor's eyes bored softly into Eve's. "I bet I deserved that," he said in a low, sexy rumble. "I bet Sean Archer is the most inattentive, sexless spouse on earth."

Before she realized it, Eve was gazing down in her lap, her head bowed. "That's not true, Sean," she said, unable to look him in the eye. He squeezed her hand.

"Of course it's true. But I'm trying to change. I'm here because I want to be alone with you. I want to see the candlelight dance in your beautiful . . ."

Castor paused. Shit. What color were her eyes? He leaned in romantically, looked at the irises which, in the darkness, were just a fringe around her dilated pupils. Brown?

". . . brown eyes," he guessed, correctly since she didn't flinch. He stood and went to her chair. He smelled her hair, her shoulders, her skin. When his fingers went to her neck, she could feel they were hot. Aroused but wary, Eve wanted to give in when Castor went for the kill.

"I . . . I wanted it all to be just right," he murmured, "when I told you about my promotion."

"What?"

He knelt before her, looking up adoringly. "It's not official yet, but it looks like Lazarro's decided to. . . retire. And guess who's replacing him?"

"Sean, that's wonderful." She was misty but still somewhat unsure. His arm was reaching up under her legs, another was around her shoulders.

"So you see, I'm not going anywhere. Unless it's . . . upstairs with you."

Overcome with rapturous emotion, Eve let her head rest against his arm. Her entire body went slack as he lifted her up firmly and strode up the dark stairs. They entered the bedroom, but Castor kept striding to the bath. He set her down gently in the shower and spun the water faucets to full, drenching her clothes.

"Sean, you're wearing your suit. . . ."

"Call me spontaneous," he purred. He pressed her against the tiles as steam filled the stall. His gritty tongue was inside her mouth when he tore off her soaked blouse. She fell to the tiles and was prostrate as he kicked off his shoes and pushed his pants down.

"Baby, it's like I'm having you for the first time," he said. And strangely, maddeningly excited, Eve succumbed to something she knew was not lovemaking, but something dark and intensely thrilling. She thanked God that Castor Troy was dead. His death had unleashed a

John Travolta stars as Jon Archer, the CMD for the West Coast Division of the National Security Agency.

Castor and Pollux (Alessandro Nivola), the brother tag team, work together in their paid mission to kill anti-drug agents.

Nicolas Cage is Castor Troy, a deadly terrorist threatening to destroy Los Angeles with a highly complex and undetectable bomb, "worse than anything God ever dumped on the Pharaoh."

Immediately after Castor plants the bomb in the Convention Center, Castor, Lars (Dana Smith, center) and Lunt (Tommy Flanagan, right) strategize.

Archer and his son Matthew just before the boy's murder by Castor, an event which ignites Archer's obsession with Castor.

After Castor escapes from Precinct, Archer chases Castor to the airport.

Archrivals finally meet, an encounter both have been awaiting for years.

Castor is "killed" at the airport hanger and the "Face/Off" begins.

Archer informs his wife Eve (Joan Allen), that against his promises, he must go on assignment again.

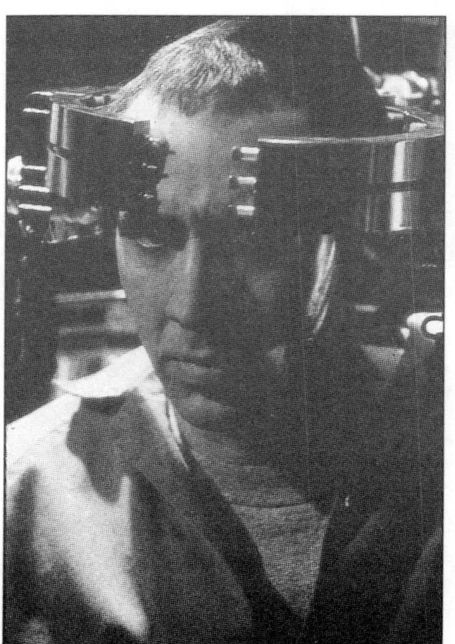

The plan gone awry, Archer, with Castor's face, is jailed, strapped down, and about to experience a brain fry.

Castor, with Archer's face, exploits the power he never imagined having with unsuspecting Hollis Miller (C.C.H. Pounder, left) and Tito (Robert Wisdom, center) in Archer's office.

Believing he is finally free, Archer finds himself trapped.

Archer escapes from jail in a desperate attempt to regain his lost identity from Castor.

gorgeous animal trapped in her husband, a beast whose churning tongue and strong fingers entered her and made her shiver in ecstasy. Castor soon unleashed his surprizing horsepower.

"All inmates are required to remove their clothing for this week's shower," was the message over the public address. Showers in Erewhon were once a week and compulsory. Archer watched the others pull off their stripes and sit naked on their cold steel platforms, waiting. When the bars to the cells opened, Archer felt strange to be wearing nothing but the steel boots. He joined the line of convicts being herded to the Hygiene Zone. They were lined up by their numbers; those who were out of place were punished with the shock stick and escorted back to their cells for three days of solitary confinement. As the line snaked through a corral of cold steel walls, Archer daydreamed of home.

"Will there by any hot water left by the time they get to us?" he asked number 2245. The man was dwarfish, with long, yellow-gray hair. One of his eye sockets was empty, and the lids over it were sewn together with black thread. "Hot water? Where do you think you are? The Ramada Inn? They got one nozzle that's gonna spray on you for thirty seconds. You won't have time to wash off your asshole."

"Will they let us take our boots off?"

"No. Never," answered the dwarf. "The only time they ever take your boots off is if they stick you in the jerky ward."

Archer considered that. "How do I get in?" he asked.

"To the Desiccation Ward? Why? They'll dry you out like a pork rind."

"Just tell me."

"Three strikes, and you're jerky." Twenty-two forty-five dropped his voice, and added, "Or else hit a guard."

"No talking," said the Filipino guard, hand poised on his shock stick. Some time later, Archer neared the end. He was pumped full of adrenaline, bordering on panic, and imagining he was going to be slaughtered for meat when he finally got to the stall. Sean wasn't surprised to see Red Walton standing nearby with a radio-wave compu-pad that entered the inmates' shower data. When a wall signal turned green, Walton hollered "Shower." Twenty-two forty-five ran into the harsh, cold spray, lifted his arms, and rubbed himself rapidly. The monitor turned red and the spray shut off. "Exit," Walton commanded.

As 2245 waddled away, Archer could see his

boots were full of water. He made a squishing noise when he walked. He joined the throng of cold, wet, towel-less inmates anxious for Archer to finish, so they could be returned to their cells and their stripes. The light flashed green.

"Shower," Walton shouted at Archer, as the nozzle spurted on. Defiantly, Archer stood outside the stall.

"You looking for trouble, Castor?"

"Yes," Archer said. In half a second, Archer's fist had made contact with Walton's chin, sending him reeling into the wall. The impact knocked Walton out, and his motionless eyes stared in different directions. The inmates were cheering as blood dripped from the side of Walton's mouth and streamed into the puddles. In an instant, the magnetic floor was activated, and all the inmates were locked down.

Archer's hand stung with pain when he opened his fist. He sensed he had fractured some bones but the ache was worth it. As a closing fence of orange-clad guards surrounded him, he raised his hands above his head, knowing what was next. The look on his face welcomed their shock sticks, which they rammed into his stomach, his spine, and his thighs. Archer shook and spasmed and convulsed, a fountain of twitching flesh, before he entered, once again, into the Little Death.

When he came back from the blackness, he was being dragged to the massive, hydraulic steel door of the Desiccation Ward. It rolled open, and for a moment, Archer was lulled by the warmth of the chamber's dry air. His eyes were drawn to the ceiling. He craned his neck to see the desiccation pods, faintly illuminated by orange light. The jerky-mates' prunelike, skeletal heads bulged with eyes both pitying and pitiful as they saw that someone else would be joining their number. Archer thought they resembled giant crickets suffocating in mayonnaise jars. The pods were suspended from the ceiling by cables, with tubes running in and out, bringing in nutrition and sucking away waste.

Adrenaline was racing through Archer as he searched the chamber. Finally, he sighted something important—high above the chamber, near the ceiling, was a viewing window of Security Central. An empty pod lowered from the ceiling. Archer feigned swooning and collapsed to the floor as they rotated the pod's glass case to face up.

The guards picked up Archer and set him in the pod. A bioengineer inserted the hypo-plugs into his arteries and activated the desiccator's dehydrate cycle. His legs and arms were left to rest outside the pod. *When are they going to take my boots off?* He felt his skin tighten as yellow fluid flowed from his body through the tubes. Finally, Archer felt his boots being deactivated. One was unstrapped and pulled off. The second one was loosened. Archer opened his eyes as he felt the tug on his second boot.

Before it was yanked off, Archer jerked his boot up hard, into the guard's chin. The second guard removed his shock stick, but Archer had already reached for the guard's shirt collar, and yanked him facedown into the glass wall of the pod. It broke into a cone of shards that gouged the guard's face. Archer pushed his face farther into the cone of glass, where it remained stuck, cutting him deeper when the guard tried to pull away. Archer kicked off the hated boot.

Without a weapon, the bioengineer cowered and backed away as Archer picked up the shock stick. Archer stunned him, turned to the desiccator, replugged himself, and reversed the machine to hydrate. In seconds, his fluids had been returned. He yanked the plugs from his body and, realizing he was naked, stripped the orange jumpsuit from the tech.

While Archer was zipping up, a deputy in Security Central turned from a game of computer blackjack to take sudden notice. He sounded an alarm, which seesawed between a low buzz and a piercing shriek. The inmates had never heard it before but sensed that someone was attempting an escape. Inside his office, Walton was still recovering from the blow Archer had landed, but, despite being groggy, he instantly leapt up and gathered a riot squad, which raced toward the chamber.

Archer saw that the door was still open. He frantically searched the wall and found the door's plunge button. He slammed it down, and the door shut. Using the shock stick as a mallet, he knocked off the button and exposed the circuitry controlling the door's mechanism. Turning the shock stick on high, he thrust its end into the mess of exposed wires and jammed the circuits. Momentarily safe, Archer knew he had nowhere to go but up.

Walton screamed orders to the Central Computer Monitor through his wrist-com. "Open the goddamned door," he shouted, and the meaning of his nickname became clear—when Walton flushed red, he turned an almost inhuman crimson. Like a broken elevator, the door opened partially, then shut again. "Shoot him!" Walton screamed, as the door spasmed once again. The guards hesitated, and the door jerked shut. Walton elbowed the other guards out of the way and, using his auto-rifle, took aim at Archer the next time the door momentarily unsealed.

Using the floor-to-ceiling matrix of support

cables, Archer dodged bullets as he climbed up and through the tangle of clear tubes channeling oxygen, food, urine, and feces into and out of the unfortunates in the pods suspended from the ceiling. A bullet burst the main urine artery which splattered.

The next time the door opened, Walton jammed the butt of his shock stick in the opening. The opening was large enough for the squad to squeeze through.

Archer reached the top of the ceiling, and, swinging out on the main food artery, he leapt onto a pod. The pods swayed as Archer crawled over them. Guards gathering underneath shot up at him, riddling the casings and bursting the tubes. Brown, yellow, and gray fluids were raining down on them, blinding them. Walton screamed as his face was besmirched. He fired aimlessly into a pod, whose glass shattered and released its inmate, who plunged on top of the guards.

The inmate's atrophied body tore apart like a broasted chicken. Arms, legs, hands, and head split off from the torso. Muddy blood from the body did not pour, but slowly seeped. The guards recoiled in horror. Walton wiped the filth from his eyes just in time to see Archer reach the last of the pods hanging before the Security Control window.

Archer took a moment to read the inmate's digital placard: PUCK, MILES M. Crime: Rape—32 convictions. Sentence: 204 years. Time remaining: 197 years, 4 months, 3 days, 2 hours, and 27 minutes. The seconds ticked away. "It's swing time, Puck," Archer said, as he rocked the pod on its cables and battered the window. It took three crashes before the thick glass gave way and shattered inward. Archer rode the pod into the booth. The deputy and security chief recoiled to the back before accepting that they had to apprehend the prisoner. The deputy pulled out his shock stick as Archer grasped for the largest shards of glass and flipped them. The glass sliced into the chest of the deputy, who screamed and folded to the floor. He turned in time to see the security chief whipping out his shock stick. Reaching for the deputy's stick, Archer saw it was set to stun and waved it like a rapier.

"C'mon," Archer said, beckoning with his fingers as he assumed the stance of a crouching tiger. The chief charged. As he began to rise from his crouch, Archer blocked the chief's stick with his own. Before the chief could reorient his shock stick in attack position, Archer brought the knob of his appropriated weapon up to the chief's shoulder and then, as hard as he could, pushed it up against his neck. The chief spasmed as the shock initiated a seizure. When he fell to the broken glass, his torso twitched, his eyes bulged, and his head slapped into the shards like a landed fish, making a bloody pulp of his hair.

Leaping to a multidimensional graphic, Archer found what he was looking for: a cross-cut diagram of the prison. It was immediately obvious that the route out was up—the graphic showed a series of chambers that stopped at a long corridor that had to be the personnel entrance. Archer was trying to figure out how to go up when he noticed the mass of cables protruding through their duct in the wall. Archer looked inside the corridor and saw he could squeeze through if he pushed the cables to one side.

Archer was shinnying upward, using the cables as guides, when he reached another corridor. This one opened into the prison's generator room. That room had a door, and after opening it, he ran through the halls past a cafeteria. He was sighted by guards, who immediately sprang to their feet. Archer knew he had to go still higher, to another level. He found a portal marked EMERGENCY EXIT SECURITY DOOR and saw a security scan-pad wired to it. He could hear the guards turning the corner. He pressed his thumb and caught his breath. The guards were getting closer. The monitor turned red and flashed PRINT UNREADABLE. Archer stuck his thumb in his mostly dry mouth and tried again.

The monitor read CLEARANCE CONFIRMED. PLEASE ENTER CODE. Archer reached for two and stopped—he was going to type in his automatic teller number.

"Christ, Archer!" he screamed at himself. He remembered Eve's birthday was 11/25 and their anniversary was 4/22. A bullet whizzed past his ear as he entered 11–25–4–22.

The guards arrived, shooting, as the door slid open. Archer threw himself into the room on the other side. It shut just before Red Walton could enter and aim his gun. He pressed his thumb to the pad as Archer took the steps in a spiraling catwalk tower three at a time. *Where am I going?* He felt like a fox being pursued by hunters—they wouldn't kill him with a bullet, but would run him down until his heart burst. In what seemed only seconds, Walton and his men entered the tower. Archer could hear the clang of the guards' feet below him, their bullets ricocheting around him as he got to a sign which read EMERGENCY EXIT ONLY, SAFTY LINES REQUIRED.

A narrow ladder was fastened to the wall, and Archer would have to leap on it. As he climbed higher, he saw a hatch outlined with light. He reached the top, pushed the hatch up, and was slapped with a great wave of salt water. He choked on it, confused, then found himself blinded by screaming daylight, by hard sunshine. Seagulls circled overhead as he crawled across a metal platform and stood. He had no time to be stunned, but stunned he was when he saw that the prison was in the middle of the ocean. He was standing, gasping for breath, on what appeared to a rusty oil rig.

What should he do? Should he throw himself into the waves and hope to swim away? What if the water was too far north and freezing and full of sharks? He turned and saw a transport chopper, the ones the guards must use to ferry to and from this hellish place every day. Could the keys be inside? Archer entered the cockpit. He looked under the seat. No keys. He flipped switches. Nothing worked.

The hatch jerked up, and Walton was the first to emerge, firing wildly. Archer backed out of the chopper and looked behind him. He could jump to a lower level on the platform and shield himself from the bullets. When he leapt, he plummeted, the two-second fall seeming to take minutes. He smacked hard on corrugated iron and rolled into a thick, high-pressure water hose. His eyes followed its length to a pres-sure valve topped with a turning wheel.

The pursuing guards had reached the edge of the upper platform and were firing on Archer even as he jerked the wheel free.

The hose came almost erect. Archer struggled to pull it into his arms. Planting his feet, he grappled with the hose as if it were a boa constrictor trying to consume him. Managing somehow to control it enough to aim it at the guards, he blinded them, knocked their weapons from their hands, and blasted several of them into the sea. The stream of high-pressure water caught Walton directly in the chest and pushed him to the platform's outer edge, where he struggled to hold on. In his peripheral vision, Archer sensed something on the water. He turned to see a tugboat pulling a Zodiac dinghy. The boats were going west into the ocean. Walton, getting a momentary respite from the inexorable pressure of the water, was climbing back from the edge of the platform and eyeing his fallen gun.

Dropping the hose, Archer ducked as it writhed wildly and stood on end, a water-gushing dragon. He made it to a pyramid of pipes, climbed up them, and bumped his head on a crane's hook. He jerked his head just in time to avoid the bullets Red Walton was firing. Archer pivoted, grabbed the hook with both hands, and kicked off the pipes. He swung over the water and, sensing the apex, let go and plunged into the sea. Instinctively, he shifted his weight to his head, straightened his legs, and dived hands first into the foaming ocean. He broke the surface doing the butterfly stroke, cutting through the waves. Bullets sliced through the water around him, and he heard their quick, wet shriek.

Waiting until the waves dipped the boat in his direction, Archer grabbed the side of the Zodiac and pulled himself up. The boat's rope to the tug was tightly wound. He freed it under a hail of bullets, pushed up the ignition switch, and roared off. He was aching to relax, but knew it wasn't over yet. As he spun the boat east, he checked the outboard engine and saw it was low on gas. How far was it to land? Twelve minutes later, land was coming into view. Through the mist he could make out the hills of San Pedro.

A shadow dropped over his head, and he panicked. He looked up to see something swooping down, then realized it was only a pelican. It dived into the water and retrieved a grunion. Archer watched the bird gobble the fish and was hungry and envious. Some freshly grilled fish would be delicious, a glass of cold water would be a miracle, and oh for a brief moment of sleep . . .

His reverie ended when the engine sputtered and died. He shrugged, picked up the oars, and began to row. His entire body ached, and he felt as if the tendons in his arms would snap. Before he could get very far, something overhead cast a shadow on the sea. But this time, whatever it was had a motor. The prison chopper made a plummeting descent, and his nemesis, Walton, face as red as a devil's, had a machine gun aimed at Archer's head. Looking at the water, Archer spotted a string of buoys. He could make out the letters of the Metro Transit Authority on them, which gave him half an idea. Dropping the all-but-useless oars, he dived into the water.

The cold water refreshed him, and he felt a sudden flow of energy to his muscles. A strange confidence filled him. He was almost relaxed, swimming six feet under ocean water, as a helicopter full of gunmen waited for his head to surface so they could shoot it full of bullets. He had outsmarted and outfought them so far, and he would do so again, but he needed to take a breath. He turned to the surface and saw the copter hovering low over the water, its blades making a circular swirl pattern. Archer knew if he swam directly into the middle of that pattern, he could take a breath and avoid the bullets. When he did so, no one saw him. He took several breaths before filling his lungs and plunging toward the closest buoy. Now he was sure why the buoys were there, what they marked.

Grabbing the buoy chain, Archer pulled

himself deeper into the sea, to a massive shadowy object. The pressure around his ears was unbearable. Walton's bullets shredded the water, but Archer went deeper until he reached the massive commuter train tube. The water was murky as he forced himself to stay under and search. Finally he found what he was looking for, a maintenance hatch painted bright yellow. Archer yanked on the latch, but his arms were weak. He needed to breathe. Conjuring the image of Castor Troy in bed with Eve, Archer tried once again and felt the latch creak up. Bracing his legs on the tube, he slowly pulled the hatch open, inch by heavy inch.

Above him, Red Walton was taking no chances. He flipped up the switch cover to the missiles and fired. The missiles were not intended for water, but wherever "Castor Troy" had gone, Walton could kill him if he was within a hundred yards of the detonation. Archer's lungs were bursting as he finally had the hatch open. The missile rocketed from the launch pod. Archer swam into the hatch as the missile streaked by. It landed on the ocean floor and detonated in a colony of abalone, sending an explosion of mother-of-pearl whipping through the water in a beautiful storm of opalescence.

Archer was succumbing to the delirium of oxygen deprivation. The water of the decompression chamber was lit up by underwater lamps. His brain was pleasantly boiling with bubbles, full of light, and he saw his wife's face before it all turned black. No longer able to contain his breath, he released it a moment before he reached the surface and took a water-drenched, lifesaving breath. Realizing he was bobbing on the surface of the water in the airlock, Archer coughed out water then breathed the sweet, precious air, taking the moment to luxuriate in oxygen. Thoroughly exhausted, he rolled on his back like an otter and floated. At the end of the chamber he saw a ladder. Summoning what little strength remained to him, he climbed to an interior door and pushed it open. Wind knocked him back. In an instant, a commuter train was speeding toward him at an insane speed, inches from his face. In another few seconds, it was gone.

Keeping his butt against the wall, he went south, figuring that was where the closest station would be. Twenty minutes later, the doors of a train opened, and passengers stared as a barefoot figure in a wet orange jumpsuit collapsed into a seat with a squish. As the train raced off Archer wondered—*How will I contact my wife?*

Chapter 10

That night, Castor tapped into Eve's sexual hunger, which seemed insatiable. By fully concentrating on her needs and pleasures, he brought her to the point where she reciprocated for him and found herself a newly devout worshiper at the altar of his sex. Later still, after they slept for a while spoon fashion, he woke her, began anew, then sent her back to sleep, happy and exhausted. Unable to sleep himself, he rose from the bed, slipped into pants and shirt, and looked down at her. He was Cortez, triumphantly gloating over Montezuma and the Aztec nation. *Use it or lose it, Sean Archer,* he thought to himself.

Leaving the bedroom, Castor sneaked a cigarette in the study. He finished reading the FBI manual, which he had brought home with him from the office, and drifted off to sleep in the study. When the sun came up, he went to the kitchen and gulped down yesterday's cold coffee. Then he finished dressing.

He was going to light a cigarette as he headed toward his car when he realized Eve was sitting on the passenger side of the Olds. He pocketed the smoke before she could see it and got in the car. She was somber, darkly dressed, and sitting properly with her purse on her lap—not the sex tigress she had been last night. It was a little spooky that she hadn't looked at him yet, hadn't said "good morning." She was staring at nothing when she finally spoke.

"Last night I thought . . ."

She paused and put on her sunglasses.

"Last night I thought, this isn't my husband."

Castor kept his eyes ahead, went icy.

"Then I woke up in the middle of the night and found you asleep in your study."

He shrugged. "I couldn't sleep. You roll around. A *lot,*" he said, and jingled the car keys. "Anyway, I'm late."

Eve thought it was strange that he was telling her she rolled around. She remembered having that conversation when they were first dating. "Sean, it's *today*," she said, and waited for him to react. He stared blankly, hoping she would clue him in. The sudden iciness of her "husband" was familiar to her, and she felt like the old Sean Archer was back.

"Sean, I know this is difficult for you, but we still have to go."

Was she dragging him to a marriage counselor? A shoe sale?

"Can't we just skip it once?" he whined. "I gotta protect and serve, you know."

Protect and serve? That's the motto of the Los Angeles Police Department, not the FBI, she thought to herself. "Protect and serve later," she spit out. "You're going."

He paused a moment. "Okay. If you insist," he said, and dropped the keys in her lap. "But you drive."

Eve drove west and turned onto the Pacific Coast Highway. They turned off on Agua Caliente into a canyon. She admired the sycamore trees growing along a trickle of a stream. After all these years, they were still such strange trees to her, a girl from the desert. They were large and crooked and growing at all different angles, as if they were ancient men trying to keep up their weak and fleshy arms. And their rough bark—it was gray and green and eighty shades in between. Castor was restless, anxious for his morning shot of nicotine. He remembered how cute Jamie looked when she smoked. He frowned when he remembered she had been out with Karl last night.

"So who's this Karl creep Jamie's been seeing?"

"Creep?"

"Yeah, creep. I get bad vibes off him. Like he's got a thing for jailbait or something."

"Charming way to refer to our daughter, Sean. He seems like a very nice boy to me. His father is a vintner. Just sold a huge piece of his land for a golf resort."

"Fine, he's rich, so what. He's still a little old for her."

"I don't know. They're about the same ages we were when we met. Remember the all-night dentist?" she asked, and smiled.

He looked at her white and pretty teeth and bared his own.

"Of course," he said. "How could I forget?" She was about to speak when he interrupted her, in need of changing the subject. His hand went to her thigh and was climbing.

"Speaking of last night, how did you like . . ."

The beeper went off. He continued to stroke her thigh, then went to nuzzle her neck and smell her hair. He ignored the beeper when it went off a second time.

"Aren't you going to get that?" she asked.

Castor pulled the beeper out, checked the number, and turned it off. His finger went to her lips, as it had last night, a prelude to other things, but now she jerked her face away. She was tense as a tightrope and a tremble was in her voice.

"Sean, really. This is hardly the time or the place." Eve felt some vague shame, the shame she felt when she first had shown her full sexuality to Sean, her ardent desire, her willingness to do the things "that good girls didn't do." Why had those feelings come back? Last night she felt deeply close to him, but this morning she felt a scary, painful distance.

The car slowed. Castor looked around, surprised to see that she had gone through the gates of a sprawling memorial park. They drove past a church and its formal gardens and headed into the upper slopes of St. Mary's-by-the-Sea. Eve had fallen into an almost trancelike silence as they wound up the twisting, turning road. When she parked, Castor waited for her to exit the car first. He had to follow her, since he had no idea where she was going.

"Come on," she said, feeling as if it was her turn to be the strong one. She offered her hand, and he left the car. They walked through the part of the park known as Land's End and continued up a bluff through a random cluster of gravestones. They could see the ocean and mist-shrouded cliffs in the distance. It was achingly beautiful, striking, and sad, and Eve's heart was full of rain. Castor stood by as she stopped at a headstone and quietly prayed. He read the etched marble stone:

MICHAEL NOAH ARCHER
BELOVED SON AND BROTHER
WE CHERISH YOU ALWAYS

Vaguely mystified, mildly stunned, Castor considered for a moment that he was different from other human beings, luckily set apart, in that he couldn't understand this woman's feelings for someone who had been dead for eight years. How could she feel so strongly after all this time? How could Sean Archer be so possessed with the memory of a dead boy that it would fuel years of obsessive hatred for his killer? Eve knelt on the grass and cleared weeds and leaves from the marker.

"Happy birthday, Mikey," she said, opening her purse. She set some toys on the grave: a little bulldozer, a rubber shark, a spaceship, a package of cherry bubble gum. When she stood, her face was stony. But suddenly she turned into Castor's body and collapsed. He held her up as she wept into his chest, weak with grief. Her sobs turned to bitter cries.

"He took our baby, Sean. He took our little boy."

Castor was annoyed. *Shut up, bitch!* he wanted to scream at her. He was holding her stiffly as he stared at the grave of a boy he had never meant to kill. *Sean Archer should never have tangled with me*, he said to himself. And then for a brief moment, a wave of something strangely painful crested in Castor Troy's breast, the feeling of loss, the pain of being a victim. For a brief moment he thought of his father's untimely death, the father he had loved and hated and eventually grown indifferent to, the father who might still be alive if he hadn't been shoved aside as negligible, drug-addicted trash by some cocky hospital interns.

Castor recalled how his father had taught his sons to steal, had rewarded them with candy and smiles and books when they brought him the means to buy heroin. Once, Castor was sniffing at his dad's stash when he was smacked upside the head. "Don't you dare!" his father had screamed at him.

"Why not?" Castor asked. He was already entering a warm and dreamy stupor. "You have enough."

"Because I don't want you ending up like me," his father said. It was the one moment Castor knew his father did love him.

Then Castor thought of Sasha Hassler, the one woman he had allowed himself to like. She fancied herself an amateur psychologist after taking a few courses at City College. She had decided that his father's death was the moment Castor had turned against humanity and forever pitted himself against authority. *Maybe that bitch had a point, but so fucking what!* he thought as waves of rage rolled through him. He had the sudden urge to strangle Sasha, strangle Eve, strangle his own mother, who he was sure was drunk on her ass before the morning game shows. Eve was still weeping in his arms when his anger took a sudden turn toward, well . . . sadness.

"Stop crying," Castor said, stroking her hair. "Stop crying . . . please."

"You picked a helluva day to leave your beeper off," said Wanda, as Castor trudged through the door, still trying to shake his funk. He didn't want to talk to her. He did want to smack her.

"What happened?" he asked.

"Castor's escaped!"

"Escaped? From Erewhon?"

She nodded. Buzz joined her and handed Archer the bulletin. Castor lurched and felt a looseness in his bowels. Wanda saw him blanch. He had been blindfolded when he was flown to Erewhon, but he knew it was only a two hour helicopter ride. Archer *had* to be in Los Angeles. He stuffed down his fear and got tough.

"I want our entire force on this," he commanded. "And alert LAPD."

"LAPD? Castor isn't stupid enough to come back to the city," Buzz said.

"Trust me. He's already here."

Buzz and Wanda stared at Castor, then turned to each other. "Move!" Castor shouted, and they scrambled off. He spun on his heel and hustled back to the parking lot.

Pollux was twitching out of control as Castor puffed frantically on his cigarette, lighting a new one off the smoldering butt. Lunt and Lars were eating wieners dipped in corn batter and sucking on lemonade. They stood under the Santa Monica Pier as Rollerbladers and bicyclists wheeled by. Occasionally, they looked back at the teenage girls wearing mod caps and hot pants in the Hot Dog On A Stick stand.

"Watch my 'wife.' He'll try to get to her first," Castor said, inflating his words with smoke.

"You want us to work side by side with the Feds?" asked either Lunt or Lars.

"Why the hell not?" Castor answered. "You're both on the payroll now. And don't fuck around. If you see him, kill him. Go."

The Swedes walked past the Cirque Du Soleil tent to their Rover. Pollux looked down at the water churning through the pier supports, then up at his brother, still not used to his strange face. "What about me? What should I do?"

"Nothing," Castor said. "People think you're a snitch. It's too dangerous."

"Like I care! I'm not just sitting here!" Pollux scratched at his ears and the temples of his head. He suddenly walked off, grinding his teeth, when Castor called after him.

"Pollux! Wait."

Pollux turned and saw the gun in Castor's hand.

"Take my Glock. It's a jungle out there," said Castor. Pollux grinned, seeing that his brother could still manage the same smirk, even with Sean Archer's face. Castor slapped the weapon into his brother's palm, and for a moment their hands locked. Pollux was warmed as he looked into his brother's dyed blue eyes.

Archer needed shoes and clothes. He rode the Metro downtown with businessmen and secretaries on their way to humdrum jobs in glass-and-steel towers. People did not stare at him. Some of them eyed him suspiciously or with mild contempt, but it was done in sideways glances. Others pretended he wasn't there. He felt the pain of being invisible and had a faint urge to scream and dance to get their attention. A proper businessman opposite him shut him out by unfolding his newspaper and using it as a screen. Archer was stunned to see a photo of "himself" on the front page. The headline read:

BOMB HERO LANDS NEW POST
Promoted to FBI's West Coast Chief

The train finally stopped at the Nickel, the corner of Fifth and Main, where the homeless and the derelicts gathered. With head down, Archer ran up the stairs of the station and walked out into the daylight. He turned into the shelter of St. Vincent de Paul's and read the handwritten name tag of Ruthe, a volunteer.

"What can I do for you, honey?" she asked. She was a real sweetheart, Archer thought, as she kept on smiling. Ruthe was an elderly widow who drove in from Encino every Tuesday to work the front desk. She was dressed in a flowery top, wearing pink lipstick, and seemed to be at ease with the mass of addicts, alcoholics, and the great unwashed around her. She set down her copy of *Chicken Soup for the Soul* as Archer tried to find words.

"Looks like you had a rough night," she said.

"I did."

"Do you need a bed for tonight?"

"No. No, thank you. But I need some clothes. And some shoes . . . I . . ."

Archer was going to lie. He was going to say something stupid, like he had lost them in a crap game when she stopped him.

"No explanations necessary," she said. "Let's see what we can do."

She led Archer into a dank, musty room loaded with racks of used clothing at very cheap prices. Archer picked out a pair of slacks, a shirt, and some shoes.

"That's two dollars," Ruthe said, and smiled again. "The money goes right back to the shelter," she added, as if he'd had suspicions that someone was actually making a profit here.

"I . . . I haven't got a dime," he told her, and looked into her eyes. He could see she was quite a looker in her day.

"You'll just have to owe me," she said. "Are you good for it?"

"You bet I am," Archer replied.

"Had your breakfast?" she asked. Archer was warmed from head to toe. He was determined to do three things: kill Castor Troy, see that Red Walton was fired and imprisoned, and send this woman a hundred roses and a fat check for the shelter. She led him to the kitchen, where breakfast was depleted, but where volunteers were assembling that day's lunch. Ruthe made him a tray and served him a lunch only slightly less sickening than the one in Erewhon. It was a sandwich of white bread, two thick chunks of oleomargarine, a single slice of baloney, and glops of mayonnaise as big as the bread. The side dish was a macaroni salad scooped from a giant wax carton. Dessert was a pile of pink-and-white-frosted animal cookies. Archer ate every bite. On his way out, he kissed Ruthe on the cheek, and she blushed and giggled as if he were a rich and handsome suitor.

It was a five-mile walk to Los Feliz from downtown. Archer's heart beat with excitement when he finally made it to Tito's street. While he was in Erewhon, he had resolved to tell all the people in his life how much he loved and treasured them. He had decided to tell Tito how much his friendship was valued, to suggest that this year they vacation together, that they start going to the gym again. Archer was sad that he would have to do it while wearing the face of Castor Troy. His heart beat faster and his shoulders tensed when he suddenly wondered if Castor had gotten to Tito. It looked like Tito was at home—Archer noticed his Saturn parked on the street. He was smiling as he trotted to the house.

Archer's heart plummeted as he sighted what

looked like yellow tape cordoning off Tito's front door. Archer looked around, didn't see any cops. A gang of teenage *cholos* noticed him as he quietly entered the backyard.

Archer pulled himself into the kitchen after forcing up a rear window. His eyes fell immediately to a chalk outline and a dried puddle of blood. Looking around the walls, he saw the bullet holes. His knees buckled, and he allowed himself to collapse. His back was against the wall as his head throbbed with rage and grief. The sensation was all too familiar. If his wife and daughter were still alive, he had to make contact now and warn them. He regained control of his breathing, went to the phone, and dialed.

"Dr. Archer, please. It's an emergency."

Archer grimaced as he heard himself. The cadence and words were his, but the voice was Castor Troy's. He clutched at his throat. The voice modulator was clipped to the cartilage of his larynx with electronic tendrils wrapped around his vocal cords. He tried to dislodge the mechanism and practiced what he was going to say.

"Hello, Eve, I know this sounds crazy but . . ." His voice scrambled into garbled static, as if it were coming from a cheap radio. When he let go of the modulator, he said, "Damn it." His voice was still Castor Troy's.

At the same time, his wife was deftly stitching together a gash above the eye of an eight-year-old girl.

Eve had allowed the youngster to cling to her Little Mermaid doll and was alarmed that the girl was so matter-of-fact about her surgery. It was the third time she had been in for this kind of cut. Eve had more than a suspicion that her injury was due to something other than falling off her Big Wheel.

"Will I still be able to wear makeup like Daddy?" she asked, and Eve stole a glance at the girl's father. He was shaved bald, with a spiderweb tattooed on his head. "Daddy" had a pierced nose with a chain that led to his ear and gobs of black mascara on his lashes. His eye sockets were puffy and black, and his pupils were dilated and glossy, like chocolate-glazed doughnuts. Eve was sure he was on something.

"Yes, honey," she said to Iris. "You can wear makeup when you grow up. There won't be any scar." Eve reached into her drawer and took out a Space Pop. She was going to ask Daddy if it would be all right to give his daughter candy when Eve realized she could probably give the girl a tumbler of battery acid without her father noticing. Eve was considering the implications of some bruises on the girl's arms when her nurse came into the room.

"Dr. Archer, your husband's on line three."

Eve left the room for the front desk and whispered to the nurse, "Get Child Services down here now—and don't let the raccoon leave." Eve picked up the phone.

"Sean? Hello?"

All Eve heard was heavy breathing at the other end of the phone.

"Hello?" she repeated. On the other end of the line, Archer was silently thanking God that she was still alive.

"Eve, listen carefully," he said. "The man you think is your husband . . . isn't."

Eve was stunned. "Who is this?" she asked.

"Please, just listen to me. Take Jamie and go to your mother's in Santa Fe. Don't tell him where you're going. Just go."

She felt as if monsters were playing Ping-Pong inside her, her heart beating rapidly. In fear, she blurted out, "Whoever you are . . . don't call again." She slammed down the phone.

Archer dropped the phone and sank into a sea of futility, his limbs taking on a sudden heaviness. He snapped back to attention when he heard a squad car's siren. Crawling to the front of the house, he peeked out the window to see the car roar into view, then continue on its way. He jumped up, energized, and went to the desk where Tito kept his gun. Bullets were there, but no weapon. He looked through the last drawer and brightened when he spotted the keys to Tito's '56 Buick, which was in the garage.

The big V-8 rumbled into life and had a quarter tank of gas. The ashtray was opened and full of coins for parking meters. Archer pressed the button to the garage door opener and was backing out when the neighborhood *cholos* jumped into his path. The leader was the tallest and the fattest and was wearing a hair net. He folded his hands menacingly on the checks of his oversize Pendleton. Archer watched them in the rearview mirror, looking for hidden weapons.

"Where are you going?" the leader asked. A tattoo on his neck said Mookie. The other *cholos* joined him, making a human fence. Archer rolled up the window and slyly locked the door with his elbow. The *cholo* standing next to the leader had a pierced tongue and pierced eyebrows. "Ten bucks he's the guy who whacked Tito," he said. Mookie jerked his head, and they surrounded the car. Archer jerked around quickly and locked the back doors.

Mookie went to the front of the car and stared menacingly at Archer, taking notes on his face, as the others pounded the windows. Archer heard the sickening creak of glass at the breaking point and floored the gas pedal. Mookie jumped on the hood just as it was backing away. As the others scattered, Mookie took hold of the wipers. Archer slammed on the brakes. The wipers snapped, and Mookie went flying, landing gut down on the pavement. As the Buick roared off, Mookie stood and shook off the pebbles which had embedded themselves in his knees. He reached for the cell phone in his chinos and dialed 9-1-1. "I want to report a stolen car, and don't put me on hold," he said.

Archer drove, determined to get to Eve. He flipped on the radio. It was an original radio with tubes in it that had to warm up before the volume gradually rose. He flipped it to KFWB, the all-news radio. When he pulled down the sun visor, a pair of sunglasses fell out. As he headed for home, a news bulletin followed the basketball scores: "Castor Troy, international terrorist and the FBI's Most Wanted Man, has escaped prison after a brief incarceration. Escapee is believed to be at large in Los Angeles and is considered extremely dangerous. If you have any information concerning the whereabouts of Troy . . ."

As he passed his home, Archer tuned out the broadcast. He made the FBI vehicles parked behind the LAPD squad cars, and was sickened to see Lars and Lunt Lindstrom, Castor Troy's Swedish meatballs, rocking in the chairs on his front porch. "God help me," he whispered. No way he could stay near here. He continued steadily past his house, neither slowing down nor speeding up. His only comfort was that Eve and Jamie might be okay with all that heat around.

Driving past the next corner, a cop car turned into the lane. Archer turned on the blinker to signal for a right and breathed a sigh of relief when the cop continued past him. As he continued driving through familiar streets and past familiar homes, they loomed before him, large and garishly bright, like solitary monsters full of parasites. He was panicking, unable to figure out where to go, what to do next. The weight of his dilemma was nearly unbearable, and he practiced his Lamaze techniques. "In . . . out . . . in . . . out." The slow breathing got his thoughts going again. *Sean—you have to think like Castor. Where would he go? Where would he feel safe, take some time out, get a hot meal?*

The answer came to him in an instant.

Chapter 11

The Buick bumped and tumbled over a roughly paved road on a run-down block. Archer had been here once before, through this sad collection of ratty boxes still serving as people's houses. In the grassless yards, roosters freely strutted among rusty car heaps sitting atop cinder blocks. A pack of skinny, flea-bitten mutts trotted through the neighborhood, stopping to peruse garbage and lick the empty boxes of TV dinners and three-for-a-dollar chicken pot pies.

He stopped at the corner liquor store, where an Asian merchant accepted food stamps and cash for the overpriced goods that were stacked on shelves behind him. He and his cash register were barricaded behind thick Lucite. Archer pointed at what he thought was a suitable and affordable gift, a bottle of Cold Duck, and dumped a fistful of quarters in a basin under the Lucite. The Asian eyed the change with contempt and averted his eyes before setting the bottle inside a Lucite cube. When he pulled a lever, a sharp electric buzz signaled Archer to open the front and take the bottle. Sean almost said "thank you," then remembered that Castor Troy had no manners.

The house was at the end of the block, which dead-ended, not in a cul-de-sac, but at a barricade that ran to the freeway. The Christopher Columbus Transcontinental Freeway sliced through the neighborhood with a violence. He could smell exhaust and felt immediately headachy from the loud *whoosh* of cars. Archer looked at the tiny bungalow, which still had Christmas decorations that had been put up sometime in the late seventies. As he approached the house, he could smell something dank and sour from the kitchen. The name, barely legible on the rusty mailbox, read HELEN O. TROY.

The screen door was off its hinges. He knocked, and an old woman, sitting in front of a black-and-white TV, reached for her dentures on a TV tray and popped them in her mouth before shuttling her bulk to the door. She was still wearing her gray hair in a late-fifties style—bangs and a ponytail. She had almost no lips in her white, puffy, splotch-riddled face, but when she saw who was on her front porch, she burst into tears. *Helen O. Troy,* Archer thought, as he looked at her for the first time in years. *With the face that sank a thousand ships.*

"My boy! My boy's come home! My baby Castor."

"Hi, Ma," Archer said, as she rammed her obese body into his own. He raised his arms as she engulfed him in her sour-smelling effluvia. The moment renewed Archer's hatred for Castor. Whoever she was, and however much she might have been responsible for the raising of a couple of psychopaths, it was obvious that Castor had completely abandoned her.

"Come in, Castor. I knew you was gonna see me sometime." Helen had seen the story on TV and had hopes that her son would take refuge with her. Every day of her life, she felt the pain of her children's abandonment, but now that Castor was here, she had a surge of happiness she hadn't felt in a decade. Archer followed her into the house, which was quite literally a dump. Old newspapers, broken furniture, clothes, cans, and bottles were piled up high, with paths cutting through them that led to important places, like the refrigerator, the television set, and the toilet. The walls and ceilings were black with smoke from the last eight decades.

"Brought you some wine, Ma," he said, and extended the bottle. Mother Troy started crying all over again.

"You want I should open this?" she asked.

"Nahh. Save it for yourself."

"You hungry, Castor? I got a pork chop on the stove I could warm."

Archer was hungry, but he could see through to the kitchen and the stove, where a pathetic pork chop lay in half an inch of congealed grease.

"No. Not hungry. I could use a lie down though."

"You just go back to your room then. I'll bring you somethin' to calm your nerves so you can sleep."

Archer wasn't sure which room was his. In one bedroom he saw some aluminum food trays scattered on the floor—their contents had been somewhat freshly consumed. Helen's collection of muumuus were piled in a corner.

He peeked into the other room and was surprised to find it clean and surprisingly well maintained, a room that was pretty much typical of a teenage boy in the seventies. On the walls were posters of KISS, Aerosmith, and Blue Oyster Cult. Somewhat incongruous was a poster of Vinnie Barbarino and the Sweat Hogs. A collection of vinyl albums sat in a bin next to an old turntable with faux-wood Con-Tact paper. He sat in a beanbag chair and heard something scrape behind him. When he looked, he found a bong in the shape of a wizard—the smoke was sucked through his pointy hat and the bowl was cradled in his fat belly, where the navel would have been. He could find nothing useful—no gun, no money, nothing.

Archer turned back the covers on a bed and undressed, looking around the room. It saddened him to remember that he had a room like this in his own house, a museum to someone's youthful memory. He opened the drawer of the night table and found a picture of Castor, Pollux, and Dietrich Hassler when they were teenagers in a band called Blow. They were dressed in seventies glam drag, and their hair was puffed into long, black perms. Archer was smiling as he looked at Castor's glitter-covered platforms. And Dietrich Hassler was wearing red lipstick and gold face paint. *Dietrich Hassler!* Archer said to himself. *I've got to contact Dietrich.*

It was almost dark when Mother Troy slipped into the room with a steaming cup on a tray and a plastic tub of something next to it.

"What are you doing there?" she asked.

"Huh?"

"Why are you in Pollux's bed?"

"Oh . . . uh, his was always more comfortable."

"Was it now? It doesn't still smell like piss, does it?"

Archer didn't know what to say. The whole house smelled like piss.

"Nahh. What did you bring me?"

"Cocoa and Kahlúa," she said, grinning lip-lessly. "Just like when you was a baby."

Archer took a sip and hoped it had all been heated to the boiling point. "You're too good to me," he said.

"Someone's gotta be good to you with that cocksucker Sean Archer chasing you all over the place."

Archer choked on the drink and turned away, smiling.

"You all right?" she asked. "You seem a little wound up."

"I'll be okay. I just need some sleep is all."

"Take your socks off," she said, and popped the lid off the tub. Archer did so, as she dunked her fingers in some white goo. "Mother will rub your feet with some sour cream and you'll fall asleep in a jiffy." Archer grinned again, in spite of all that had happened, and allowed her to massage his toes with some Jerseymaid. She was looking fondly at the Sphinx etched onto his ankle. It wasn't exactly an accurately detailed drawing since the lion-woman's lips were red and full and modeled after those of Marilyn Monroe.

"Ahh, Castor. I remember the day you stole our rent money to pay for those tattoos, the Seven Wonders of the World." She looked at her "son" and smiled, content to see he had fallen asleep. "And you was gonna be the eighth," she whispered, convinced that he was.

Archer slept through to the afternoon and woke up after having the Dream. It was the exact same fox hunt in the sky, except that this time, Archer was stuck with Castor's face when Michael vanished in his arms. Still, he was almost refreshed after a full night's slumber, and, with a clear mind, he calculated a strategy. He allowed Mother Troy to serve him some coffee in a somewhat less than clean mug, and declined the second offer of the pork chop. It was at that moment that she shrugged, picked it up, and ate it herself, gnawing the meat off the bone. He boiled a few nearly rotten eggs and ate them while she watched a women's boxing match. When twilight neared, he told her he had to go.

"Be careful, Castor," she said, and started to cry. She knew she might never see him again. "You tell Pollux to come see me."

"We'll both come," Archer said. "We'll go out for dinner."

"That'd be swell," she said. It had been decades since she'd been to a restaurant.

He left wearing a baseball cap to obscure his head. In a matter of minutes, he would be out of this sad neighborhood south of the freeway and smack in the glitz of Beverly Hills.

Jamie had skipped school so Karl could take her to Tijuana to get her another tattoo. First he got her drunk, something teenagers could easily do just south of the border, and so far, she had let him pay for everything. They had eaten grilled lobsters, downed many margaritas, and, like all the frat boys around them, they were doing "poppers" at Señor Frog's. Waiters slammed a combination of soda, tequila, and root beer schnapps on the table, and then pressed the glass to the customers' mouths with a dirty rag. Foam exploded, ran through their noses and down their throats, as the waiters shook the drinkers' heads.

The tattoo artist was a young guy who worked shirtless. His brown torso was covered with re-creations of the murals of Diego Rivera. Jamie pointed to the tattoo she wanted, a triple portrait of the original Charlie's Angels. She wanted it on her butt cheek, where her parents couldn't see it. Karl enjoyed the view as she pulled down her tight little shorts. She rolled up a bandanna and bit down on it as the tattooist went to work. Karl was aroused. He had already picked out a motel for them on the American side and anticipated getting a handjob while waiting in the car at the border crossing.

Dietrich Hassler looked with contempt at the latest series of paintings, from a Korean artist, being hung in his gallery. Parisian critics had unanimously dubbed him the most "important new presence in the post non-representational movement." Dietrich figured he was sleeping with all the right people. His paintings were almost all the same, a series of black stripes that were wide and narrow and alternated with gray or white. Within the stripes were small pen or pencil strokes, and planted in at least one of the stripes was a small, crude drawing of an insect. One of them had already sold for three hundred grand to someone who procured for Atlantic Richfield. *Fine by me,* Dietrich thought, as he left for the day, locking the back door and heading toward his Lexus.

His attention was drawn immediately to a forensics team swarming over a '56 Buick parked down the street. Dietrich averted his face and hastened to his car when he realized that leading the team was that asshole "Sean Archer."

"Some poor schmuck's in trouble," Dietrich mumbled to himself, as he backed out of his spot and onto the street.

"Yeah . . . me" said Archer, hunkered down in the back of the Lexus.

Dietrich slammed on the brakes and snapped a pistol from inside his jacket. He jerked around and brought it to the face of "Castor Troy." He exhaled as a car honked at his Lexus blocking traffic.

"Jesus Christ Almighty, Castor. I just about shit my pants."

"Drive. And punch up your cellular. I need you to make some calls," said Archer, as the Lexus continued into traffic and away from the forensics team.

"Where do you want to go?" Dietrich asked.

"Where do you think I want to go?" he barked. "I'm a fugitive."

"I dunno. My place?"

"Yes, your place. Get Fitch and Aldo on the phone."

The Lexus reached the patchwork of industrial buildings and vacant lots east of Little Tokyo. They rolled over train tracks and past a rail yard to a cluster of brick buildings. Dietrich steered to the subterranean parking lot of a building where silk stockings and parachutes had been manufactured. They took a freight elevator to the top floors, where Dietrich lived in an enormous, splashy loft. At the top of the loft was an attached structure that contained Dietrich's spacious bedroom. Next to the loft's living space was a large and sunny rotunda which served as a gallery for his private collection.

The loft itself was full of paintings and sculptures, many of which he had stolen from himself in order to collect the insurance. Some giant Oldenburg sculptures were in the main chamber, and they were the first thing Archer saw when they stepped through the steel security doors.

The first of the soft sculptures was a gargantuan frying pan with eggs and bacon in it. The bacon was big enough to be a mattress. The other Oldenburg was a giant bowl of alphabet soup with letters as big as throw pillows. Archer checked out the art as Dietrich climbed up a spiral staircase to his bedroom. On the wall below the bedroom entrance was a painting the size of a large movie screen. It was an impressive portrait of Castor's gang. Archer saw Sasha's signature at the painting's bottom, where she had done a self-portrait of herself at a canvas. Archer looked up at the ceiling, which was covered with skylights. He had never been able to get into this loft, and now that he had seen it, it irked him that his enemy's friends lived so well.

Upstairs, Dietrich gave his head a quick shave, then returned with some drugs. He thought "Castor" was strangely quiet and offered him the chance to coke up.

"Maybe later," Archer answered as he looked at the video monitors of the building's entrance and the streets outside. Fitch and Aldo were arriving in a stretch limo. Four bodyguards stepped out first, and Archer recognized one of them, a promising tailback who had played for the 49ers before his knee was wrecked. Now his head was shaved, and he was wearing what looked like gold chain link on his nearly naked chest. He held open the door, and some young and beautiful women appeared. Sean made them as Livia Durgenschott and Cindee Cuppens and was somewhat surprised they hadn't been shed yet since women in Castor's crew had a high turnover rate. Their clothing was expensive but sleazy, and they looked both sexy and tough as they smacked on chewing gum. Fitch and Aldo finally stepped out.

Sean went to the bathroom to get ahold of his nerves. He splashed cold water on his face as Dietrich let the guests in.

"So what's the big surprise?" Aldo asked Dietrich, as the girls went to the bar and made drinks. Overhearing Aldo, Sean told his mirror image, "You are Castor Troy. This is *your* old crew. You don't take shit, and you don't take no for an answer."

Puffing up his chest, Archer strutted out and slammed the door behind him. He strode over the glass-bricked floor and watched Aldo and Fitch stiffen in shock. Livia and Cindee beamed, forgetting their cigarettes, as ashes dropped on the floor.

Fitch finally found his tongue and stared at Archer in rage. "Are you crazy? You're going to bring the Feds down on all of us!"

"Archer doesn't want you, he wants me!" Archer shot back. "But I'm going to get him first . . . with your help."

"Forget it," Aldo said. "You're radioactive." He turned to leave, signaling the others to follow. Archer sprang at him, wheeled him around, and smashed him into the wall. Aldo tried to grab his gun, but Archer had already stripped him of it. He pivoted to face the bodyguards, who had surrounded him on three sides and drawn their weapons.

"You wanta face off with Castor Troy?" Archer shouted, his voice reverberating through the loft. "Come on, then! Come on, 'cause I've had a real bad day!"

He looked around and saw that all the

bodyguards were sweating. Aldo and Fitch were transfixed by fear. Cindee and Livia were smiling, feeling hot for "Castor."

Archer stared hard into Aldo's eyes and pushed the gun into his chest.

"You dumb fucks are forgetting who the real enemy is," Archer said. He was starting to enjoy himself, like an actor gaining a sudden insight into his character in the middle of a performance. Then he slowly, genuinely smiled. He let the gun drop from his palm and it swung on his trigger finger before he slipped it back into Aldo's vest. The tension eased up.

"Three years ago, Sean Archer hauled you in for questioning," he said to Aldo, who was blinking involuntarily. "He rattled you so bad, you shit your Armani suit right there in the interrogation room." Aldo's blood-drained face suddenly flushed red and was beaded with sweat. *How does Castor know that?* he wondered. Fitch burst out laughing, a crude, piercing howl, and it cut through Aldo's gut. He wasn't sure who he hated more at the moment, Fitch or "Castor." Archer turned to Fitch and sneered.

"You laugh, Fitch. The way Archer laughed at your last arraignment, in May of '94, when you got down on your knees and tried to blow your way to freedom."

Fitch cringed as everybody cracked up. If he

had had a pickax, he would have buried it in "Castor's" face and watched it exit from the back of his head.

"We all have a reason to hate Sean Archer. We all want to see him dead," Archer ranted, sensing he had consolidated his power. "This is our chance."

Dietrich nodded in agreement. "Tell 'em what you've got in mind, Caz," he said.

Archer relaxed and lit a cigarette. He was starting to like the little puffs of poison and sucked in the smoke like mother's milk. "We start with your basic kidnapping. Then . . . a little surgery."

"Surgery?" Fitch asked. He was imagining a long, slow mutilation of Sean Archer's face and body.

"Yeah. I'm going to rearrange his face in a way you won't believe."

"You're an evil bitch, Caz," said Aldo, smirking. "But you've got balls of titanium."

Fitch and Aldo both slapped an arm around Archer. "Count us in," Aldo said. Archer puffed on his cigarette and exhaled the smoke in a sigh of relief. *You did all right,* he thought to himself, as Dietrich plucked a gold-and-enamel box from his jacket and produced a blue gelatin capsule. The others smiled as Dietrich turned to the bar and cracked open the capsule, letting the powder sift into a big highball glass. He doused the powder with mescal, and, with the last drop, the worm rushed out. *Not again,* Archer thought, as Dietrich stirred the mixture.

"How about one of your famous toasts, Caz?" Dietrich asked, as he handed the glass to Archer.

Archer froze. In the silence, everyone turned expectantly toward him. Nothing came to mind. He raised his glass. "Uh, to old jobs, new jobs, and . . . uh . . . blow jobs?"

The toast fell like a turd. Then Dietrich snickered, followed by Fitch, Aldo, and the rest. The laugh was coming more in reaction to the previous tension, but the girls and bodyguards joined in. Archer drank down the cocktail in a swallow and wiped his mouth on the back of his hand. He chewed up the worm, like he'd done in prison, and slowly turned to each of them with the pulp at the end of his tongue. Everyone laughed all over again.

"Enough business, Caz. We wanna dance," said Livia as she punched up some trance music on the disc player. On an empty stomach, the liquor nearly crashed into Archer's system. The effect brought with it the beginning of some other sensation that would soon surpass the alcohol. Livia took Archer's hand and brought him to the glass-bricked floor. Cindee flipped a switch and colored lights from underneath the bricks ebbed and flowed. As the Quantrex kicked in, Archer felt he was those lights, as if his solid human body had become the lights' lingering phosphorescence.

Cindee joined Livia, and they sandwiched Archer with their taut bodies, doing a slow grind. Archer was dancing, losing all stiffness, and feeling darkly entwined with the music's somber throb. He was vaguely aware of a warm, cupping sensation and looked down to see Cindee rubbing him. She looked up at him, opened her mouth, and clamped her lips over his. When her champagne-stained tongue drove into his mouth, he felt as if his entire body had been penetrated by something moist and fiery and tart. Livia was slowly running her hands over his backside. Archer plunged into the sensations of asphalt being smoothed by a steamroller. She turned him around and thrust her martini-coated tongue in his mouth. His mind reeled in a grove of blossoming lime trees, and he tasted and identified all eleven flavorings of Bombay gin—juniper was the strongest, and anise was the weakest. When Livia spoke to him, he felt like he was looking into a blowup of her face, as if she were in close-up on a giant movie screen.

"Remember the Chargers' game, Caz? The owners' box? We did it four times."

Though Archer hadn't been there, he was almost sure he could remember making love to this girl. Outside the owner's box, a crowd originally gathered to watch football had turned their attentions to cheering for them, for their ecstatic sex. The crowd had doffed their own clothes to give them a nude "wave." From inside his pants, Archer felt a strange, yet familiar sensation. He was sure that inside his boxer shorts, a thousand topless French women, the size of ants, were erecting the Eiffel Tower.

"Sure I remember," Archer slurred. "Once a quarter, right?" Archer panicked when he realized he had a sudden and terrible urge, but what urge was it? Did he have to piss? To shit? No. When he closed his mouth, he thought it was full of sand, rocks, and cacti. He realized he was deadly thirsty and staggered past the giant frying pan, which spread as vast as a parking lot. He stumbled past some giant abstract paintings, which seemed to be reaching out with twisted, paint-splattered arms to tear at him. Reaching a short staircase that went to the kitchen, he slid on his ass to the bottom of the steps. The chrome tap was the most glittering, beautiful object in the universe, as he rushed toward it, stuck his head under, and drank greedily. Archer stopped to breathe and saw a woman's reflection in the sink's window. She had arms angrily folded over her chest. Was it real? He emerged from his watery paradise to see Sasha Hassler. Her image registered, and for a moment he felt like a computer gathering data from its memory banks.

"Sasha Hassler," he said. "Age, 35. Met Castor Troy in Austin, Texas, at a Pearl Jam concert." Suddenly Archer caught himself, feeling as if he were beating back the ocean's waves.

"Uh, how ya doin', baby?" he asked.

Her hand opened. The meat of her palm swung back and landed with a sharp smack on his cheek. Archer felt like the city of Hiroshima just after it had been bombed.

"What the hell are you doing here? You're supposed to be dead," she said. As he stared at her, he saw her speaking from inside a mushroom cloud. Suddenly everything went black. Archer envisioned a city of wood-and-paper houses being flattened by the megaforce of an atomic whirlwind. Sasha watched him wobble, then fall flat on his face. He had entered once again into death within life. Dietrich stepped into the kitchen, alerted by the thud, followed by the others.

"Well!" Dietrich exclaimed. "When Castor Troy can't handle a little Quantrex, that, dear friends, is the first sorry whiff of old age."

□ ■ □

Karl's balls were as blue as a navy uniform. The little bitch had rejected his offer to spend the night at a Motel 6. He didn't get a hand job. She wouldn't even let him kiss her. He'd bought her some silver skull earrings just after they left the tattoo parlor and a piñata in the shape of the Tick. What else did she want?

Jamie had played with the radio all the way up from San Diego, searching for the songs she liked, and to avoid talking to Karl. Her bottom was raw and itchy from the tattoo. She felt uncomfortable with him, and especially uncomfortable about asking him to pull over when she had to pee. He was feeling cheated, as if he had dumped a pile of cash on a campfire and hadn't even roasted a marshmallow. She was a hot little piece of snatch, but she wasn't that hot with all her tattoos and trendoid clothes and makeup. He'd never had the intention of taking her home to meet his parents, they would have freaked. If she was going to dress that way, she should put out, the little tease. Nobody held out on Karl Gustaffson after he had dripped all that honey. And now they were almost at her house.

Castor stood on the balcony of the Archer home looking out over the city lights. Where was that fuck-pig Archer hiding? He lit his last cigarette and realized he'd gone through four packs that day—he was hacking. His eyes searched the inverted star field of the Los Angeles Basin. The dark blue and starless sky above was filled with vaguely orange mist. His thoughts on Archer's whereabouts led nowhere, and that made him even jumpier. Castor wanted to shout his frustration into the night sky, wanted to kill someone. His violent ruminations were interrupted when he recognized Karl's BMW purring up the all-too-quiet street. Castor would know from the look on Jamie's face whether the Karl creep had boinked her.

She was breathing a sigh of relief as the car finally reached her house. She gathered up the piñata and other souvenirs. "Thanks for all the stuff and food and everything, Karl. I had, ummm, a good time." She rolled her eyes and, staring straight ahead, offered her hand for a shake. *You little fucking bitch,* he thought. Taking her hand, he pulled her face to his mouth and kissed her. She succumbed to one closed-mouth kiss and pulled away. His arm dropped over her shoulder, and he roughly pulled her tighter, his tongue vulgarly slithering over her face.

"Karl, no. Karl . . . cool it."

From the balcony, Castor could see that Jamie was resisting Karl. Castor quietly trotted down the back stairs and crept to the garage gate to get a closer look. Then he could see Karl had gone animal and was pawing Jamie, licking her mouth.

"Karl! Stop it," she said, trying to open the door. He knocked her hand away and leapt on top of her. His hand reached for a button on the seat's side, and it lowered back.

"Listen," she shouted. "My father's got a gun and he'll . . . he'll . . ."

Karl had jerked his belt open and pushed down his pants. "That wimp won't do shit," Karl said as he pulled at her shorts. "And you said he's never home."

Glass exploded. Crystal pebbles rained on Karl's half-naked body. Jamie screamed. Karl turned to see Castor's shoe being pulled back through what had been the passenger window. Now Castor's hands were in the car and reaching into Karl's scalp. He yelped as Castor jerked him by his hair, over the broken edge of glass, out of the car, and up into an enraged face.

"Who are *you* to call Sean Archer a wimp?" he snarled, as Jamie sprang from the car. Castor grabbed Karl by his polo shirt and heaved him hard into the windshield, spiderwebbing it. Karl rolled off the hood and to the ground, the wind knocked out of him as he rose. Desperate to take a breath, he grew more frightened when he saw Castor drawing his arm back for a jab. Karl ducked and somehow managed to get into the front seat, making the wheezing sounds of an asthmatic as he turned the key. The Beamer crept away as Jamie ran in the house.

Castor entered the living room to see Jamie bound up and rocking in the corner of the sofa. She wouldn't look at him.

"What are you—stupid?" he asked.

She looked at him in disgust and burst out in tears. "That's—just—like you!" she shouted through sobs. "Some guy tried to rape me, and you side with *him.*"

Castor's head shifted back and forth in disbelief. "Did it look like I was siding with him?"

She stared at the floor.

"Did it?" he shouted. "You wanna play with some scummy organ grinder, then you better be prepared. Do you have protection?"

Ick, she thought. She was not going to have *this* discussion with her *father.* Her mouth screwed up tight before she said, "You mean like . . . condoms?"

"I mean like *protection,*" Castor answered. With a fluid motion, Castor reached into his pocket and expertly snapped open a well-oiled switchblade. He handed it to Jamie. Astonished, she stared first at the blade, then at her "father."

"For me?"

"Next time, slip it in low, then twist it. So the wound doesn't close."

Jamie took the blade and practiced unsheathing it. Castor corrected her until she had the basic technique.

"You'll pick up speed later," he said. "Now, uh, brush your bed and go to teeth. It's a school night."

Jamie looked at him admiringly and suddenly lunged to hug him. Completely flustered, he didn't know what to do until it occurred to him to hug her back. She finally let go and kissed him on the cheek before dealing with her own embarrassment, then ran up the stairs. Castor rubbed his cheek and picked up his keys to go buy smokes. *No wonder he spent all his time chasing me,* he thought. *Who can deal with this family shit?*

He was almost out the door when the phone rang.

"Sean Archer."

"It's me, bro," wheezed Pollux, "with my eyes glued on the real Sean Archer."

"Where is he?"

Pollux was across the street from Dietrich's loft in an abandoned parking structure. He was using night-vision goggles to watch Sasha put Archer to bed.

"I thought he might visit some old friends of yours," Pollux said into his cellular. "And Castor, if I didn't know better, I'd swear that dork-suck *likes* being you."

Chapter 12

Archer was coming back from blackness to a softly lit room. Where was he and where had he been? He remembered something about Hiroshima and Sasha Hassler and drinking a lot of water. He realized his pants were wet and smelly and someone was tugging them off. It was Sasha, and he gathered from the feminine touches and lithographs of Frida Kahlo and Georgia O'Keeffe that he was in her bedroom. He covered himself as best as he could with his shirttail and noticed she was clad in a nightie. She was searching through her drawer for something—condoms?

"Uh, can't we just talk?" Archer asked.

"Talk? The only talk I ever heard from you was 'take it off,' 'sit on it,' and 'I'll pay you tomorrow.' Here," she said, and pulled out some fresh Castor-style clothes and dumped them on top of him. "Take off your homeless outfit and get dressed. Then get out," she said, neatening the drawer.

"Not until I finish my business with your brother," he said, manufacturing some toughness. He climbed into the silky black trousers. They felt like he was wearing nothing at all.

"Make it snappy. If Sean Archer finds out I've seen you . . ." She turned to him, looked him in the eye, and said, ". . . I'll lose my son." She looked down at the floor, her shoulders hunched in fear. Something pleading was in her brief moment of eye contact. Archer realized for the first time that he wasn't dealing with a hardened felon, but a frightened, protective mother. He had the sudden realization of the effect his own relentless obsession had had on Sasha. Unconsciously, he slipped into himself as he made her an apology.

"I know I've done some things that have made your life hard . . ." he began. She turned on her heel and machine-gunned her words at him.

"How would you, Castor? You walked out on me without even leaving a Post-it."

Castor. I'm Castor, he remembered. "I'm not the same person you remember, Sasha. And for what it's worth . . . I'm sorry."

She turned away from him again, pretending to look for something in the drawer. Her back tensed. Inside her, she was chasing away remnants of love with the wild dogs of her hatred. She suddenly softened when her son came running into the room to his toy bin. He knelt before it and took out some Power Rangers and their Zords. Archer was halfway through buttoning his shirt when he stopped, instantly captivated by the boy. Sasha took note of "Castor's" strange reaction, and Archer finished buttoning. He looked in the mirror at his clothes. The shirt was Italian, olive-colored with gold threads running through it. It was something he would never have worn. It probably would have cost him a week's salary to buy it. "Not a bad fit," he said, thinking that the face finally matched the clothes.

"They should fit," she said. "They're yours." It took Archer a moment to figure out the poignancy of what she had said. She had not seen him in years, but she still held on to his clothes. *What can she possibly love about this man?* He watched as she turned her focus to her son, who was inserting the Yellow Power Ranger into the Tiger Zord.

"Nice-looking kid," he said.

"Of course he is, Castor. He's . . ." She held back what she wanted to say, something that caught in her throat because hours before, she was sure that Castor was dead. She'd better say it now.

". . . he's yours, too," she choked out, and shyly turned to look at him. She was surprised to see him react at all, and doubly surprised when he paled in shock.

Archer and Sasha were unaware that their silhouettes were under heavy scrutiny from Castor and "his" team. Buzz, Wanda, and Loomis were atop the roof of the parking structure opposite the loft. Wanda turned occasionally to watch Castor quietly converse with Pollux. As she rechecked her rifle, she looked at the two of them and felt that an all-too-facile cooperation had emerged between Archer and the man who had once been his second greatest enemy. *What other plot is Pollux hatching with his IQ of 197*? she wondered. The other agents were equally suspicious, but only Loomis, the rookie, had had the nerve to ask "Archer" why he was so sure that Pollux would set up his own brother. "I've never been more certain of anything in my life," Castor had said.

Castor scurried back to the agents, assuming Archer would leave once he had tied his shoes. "Everyone in position," he whispered loudly.

"And remember, shoot to kill." Loomis and Buzz indicated their objection to the order with the drooping of their firearms, but Castor's steely eyes said, *Don't argue. That's an order.*

Buzz exhaled, steeled himself, and said, "You heard the boss. Let's saddle up." The agents spread out in positions along the roof. Castor, naturally, had chosen the spot where he could fire the first fatal shots at Archer. Wanda heard the footsteps of someone leaving the roof and turned to see Pollux trotting away. Where was he going, and why was "Archer" allowing him to leave?

The real Archer was coming back from the news that the boy who had been charming him was the offspring of his hated enemy. "How old is he?" he asked, as he laced Castor's tight shoes. His and Castor's feet were a half size different.

"Five," Sasha answered, feeling both relief and regret that the secret was out. Would Castor want to raise him now, have rights to him, want to drag him into a life of chaos, global mischief, and riches drenched in blood?

"No one knows you're his father," she said.

"Why not?"

"I thought someone might want to hurt him. Just to hurt you."

"Bang, bang, bang," said Adam as he picked up a clear plastic ray gun and aimed it at them. The boy flipped the switch on the gun. Lights inside of it blinked as it emitted a series of annoying ray-gun sounds, like those car alarms that progress through a series of different sirens. Startled, Sasha took it from his hands.

"You know Mommy doesn't like you playing with those things," she said, and dropped it back in the bin. He didn't understand her feelings and pouted. She lifted him up, then urged him in Archer's direction.

"Adam, this is your father," she said. The boy stared at the ground when she nudged him. "Go on. Go to him," she lightly urged, and he looked into Archer's eyes as he toddled over and raised his arms. Archer's left eye twitched as he awkwardly took the boy. His big hands dwarfed the boy's body. Archer was drifting away as an avalanche of emotions overloaded every nerve. Tears welled, and he was breathing hard. Adam strained in his tightening arms.

"You're not holding him right, Caz. Caz?"

Sasha could see he had left, but had no idea where he had gone. The calliope music was back in Archer's head: every note of "Camptown Races" was a blistering jab as he sat on Pegasus and whirled forward in a dizzying circle. He heard Mikey's laughter, saw the red balloon, and jumped when the memory of the gunshot tore through his brain for the ten thousandth time. Archer came back, loosened his grip on Adam, and the boy relaxed. He was in the thrall of being in someone's strong arms, the arms of an adult male, and he felt a strange comfort unlike anything he had known in his short life. The feeling made Adam smile. Archer was torn between fatherly affection for the boy and his own terrible loss. His body stretched to its fullest, and his shoulders squared as he thrust the child back into Sasha's arms.

"This is not my son," he said. Sasha was angered by what she had to reckon was his complete denial.

"Yes, he is!" she hissed. She turned her son away, to shield him from the cruelty of this man who was looking blankly out the window at the night. She looked over her shoulder at him with her usual contempt when she saw him suddenly go rigid.

He was alerted by some shadowy glimmer on the opposite rooftop. Next he vaguely heard a metallic clicking. The hairs rose on Archer's neck. Adrenaline flooded his system.

"GET DOWN!" he screamed, and hit the floor. When Sasha hesitated, he reached for her ankles, jerking her and her son to the carpet, pulling them against the wall. A half second later the windowpanes shattered. Gunfire riddled the loft, shredding the walls and paintings, splintering the furniture.

On the parking structure's rooftop, agents firing their weapons were posted opposite each of the loft's windows, and all of the glass had exploded. Loomis aimed into each broken window with a grenade launcher. The grenades burst and flooded the rooms with tear gas. The others continued their fire.

In the living room, two of the bodyguards were playing canasta when a stream of bullets shot up a glass table. It burst into shards that exploded into their bodies and faces. The former tailback took a bullet in his knee and fell forward. He took a second bullet in the middle of his shaved head. The other one ran, pulling a dagger of glass from his leg.

Fitch had been fucking Cindee on the kitchen counter as a hail of bullets pinged on the hanging cookware. They ricocheted in a deadly whirlwind around the steel-paneled room. The bottle in the water dispenser ripped open.

Fitch and Cindee slid to the wet ground and sheltered behind the stove as a grenade smashed into the refrigerator, exploded, and released its volatile gas. Fitch choked as he found his gun in his clothes.

In Sasha's bedroom, Archer took advantage

of the roiling smoke to slither out the door on his stomach. He was almost in the hall when he heard Sasha. "Adam!" she screamed. Her wail of fear froze Archer. He turned and saw the child trying to rise, choking on the tear gas, his face a silent scream. The gunfire had lapsed.

"KEEP FIRING!" Castor screamed. Archer heard him and, through the window, saw his enemy's figure rise, holding a machine pistol. A spray of automatic fire was coming through the window, and the line of bullets was fast approaching Adam.

As Archer stared at his worst enemy's child, he was ripped apart by two impulses. Like a toad, Archer suddenly jumped at the boy. He was pulling him into his arms under the window when a snouted figure rappelled in through the broken glass. The SWAT agent's weapon was poised, and his finger was beginning to squeeze the trigger when Archer kicked him hard in the crotch. He fell forward in pain as Archer's shoe made contact, this time under the chin. The impact sent the agent, still attached to his rappelling gear, flying out the window, where he plummeted until his ropes jerked, preventing him from smashing to the ground.

Adam screamed and clamped his hands over his ears aching from the din. Archer reached for Sasha's Walkman, pressed the ON button, and slipped the headphones over the boy's head. His ears were filled with Judy Garland singing "Over the Rainbow." Archer grabbed the boy and curled him into his body before scrambling with him out the door. Sasha was in the hall and jerked on Archer's shirt. "This way," she shouted, leading him into a large closet. She began kicking at the plasterboard, and Archer helped her. When the hole was big enough, they entered a narrow corridor filled with pipes and vents. There was just enough room to negotiate the corridor.

Fitch and Cindee sputtered in agony on the kitchen floor, coughing up blood and mucous, which dotted the tiles. Anytime they approached the door, they were shot at. When the tear gas receded, Fitch stepped to the side of the window to aim his gun just as a SWAT agent on a swinging rope barreled through. His feet landed in Fitch's face. Fitch was laid out, with his hand quivering, when the agent snapped out his gun and fired into his chest.

Cindee reached through the debris and sprang up with a meat cleaver. The agent's first bullets caught her shoulders, nailing her back against the refrigerator. The next three bullets were buttons that entered in a straight line down her chest. Her corpse slumped as SWAT agents succeeded in blowing out the front door with fuel-air explosives. The agents swarmed through the loft in their hoods and gas masks, an army of black locusts.

Dietrich, in his underwear atop the spiral staircase, leapt into the doorway of his bedroom to counter the invasion with an AK-47. He opened fire, and the front line of agents collapsed. The rest retreated through the front door, back onto the street, as Archer, Sasha, and Adam emerged from the utility closet. They were running across the glass-bricked floor when they heard the screeching crash of the skylight bursting above them. A new swarm of agents were invading, scooting down their rappelling lines likes water bugs, firing before they touched the ground.

Aldo and his bodyguard were hunkered behind the bar as the agents converged. The bodyguard peered out to fire. The first bullet hit him in the hand, sending fingers flying and his Glock spinning away. The next caught the top of his head and sliced just under his skull. When it emerged from the back of his head, it spattered Aldo with blood and brain cells. Aldo made his break for the spiral staircase, passing through the hail of bullets.

Archer pushed Sasha and Adam behind the massive couch as a squat, muscular agent dropped to the floor just in front of him. Archer sidestepped the invader and jabbed a fist into his arm, sending the gun flying toward the couch. The two men tangled. The agent freed himself with a blow to Archer's face that momentarily stunned him and moved to where the gun lay on the floor.

Just as the agent reached for it, a tiny foot kicked it away. While the agent was looking up at Adam's determined little face, Sasha sprang out from behind them. She scooped up the gun and smashed the butt end into the back of the head of another plummeting agent. She fired, and the bullet tore through the rope of a third invader who fell, facedown, knocking himself unconscious. Archer recovered just as the squat agent turned on Sasha.

Leaping on the man's back, Archer knocked him down. The force jerked the gas mask from his head. Archer looked into the angry, frightened face of a friend. "Buzz!" he said. Hours later, Buzz would wonder why Castor Troy had called him by his first name. At the moment, he felt nothing but fear and hatred.

The sight of Castor's face sent adrenaline coursing through Buzz's system. He reached for the knife in the holster on his thigh and was about to jab it into Archer's side when Archer managed to knock the weapon under the couch. Wanting Buzz out of the way, but determined not to kill him, Archer lifted Buzz and heaved him through the glass doors of the dining area. Buzz was lying in the glass pebbles of the door, twisting like a tortured insect, when more SWAT agents rushed through the front. Archer looked up at the giant painting and saw Dietrich standing over it with his machine gun.

"Dietrich! The painting!" Archer shouted, and Dietrich understood instantly. Pointing down on the top of the canvas, he fired, cutting loose the painting. It collapsed, to billow and enshroud the latest wave of invaders. By creating this brief interruption, Dietrich had bought them some time.

"Let's go!" Dietrich yelled, as Sasha, Archer, and Adam hustled up the staircase.

"Shoot!" Castor shouted into his walkie-talkie. He was commanding a third wave of agents, who were swarming under the glass floor of the loft.

Adam stumbled at the third step of the staircase and fell back on the glass-bricked floor. The agents had weapons trained on the fallen "target" above them. "Shoot them for fuck's sake!" Castor screamed on their headsets. Archer yanked Adam away just as a geyser of glass exploded upward. Adam heard nothing but Judy Garland bleating about "happy little bluebirds." Archer was caught in the fringe of the explosion, but pulled Adam to safety on the stairs. As they spiraled to the top, agents under the floor fired blindly. From his bedroom, Dietrich fired down into the hole.

From outside the windows, the SWAT team consolidated their control of the building. They had killed Livia and a bodyguard who had sneaked away for some recreational sex in the sauna. Now the agents poured in like army ants returning to their nest. Archer led his "family" into Dietrich's bedroom, where Aldo and the last bodyguard were waiting. Reaching under some blond wood paneling, Dietrich pulled at a hidden door, and said, "If we make it, we'll meet you up at the Topanga place. You better move, Caz."

Archer gave the slightest nod and handed Adam to Sasha. She hugged her son and, with a free arm, reached for Archer, hugging him as tightly as she could. She knew it was over for him. Nothing less than a direct intervention by Satan could save her man. The net was tightening, and the metallic clank of boots was rising up the stairs.

"Thank you, Caz. Thank you," she said.

Archer broke away, gave her a slight push into the hidden compartment, and said, "Take care of your son." Dietrich pointed Archer to the door of the rotunda. Archer ran to it as the agents appeared. Dietrich and Aldo tried to hold them off, hoping to follow Archer, but the agents let loose a withering fire that a force twice as large could not have withstood. The two men fell, and their bodies shook as they were shredded by automatic fire.

Archer emerged on the top of a staircase in the private gallery of the rotunda. Moonlight shone through the skylight, giving a silver illumination to the sculptures and paintings. Archer heard the unfiltered scrambling of the agents from a far window and realized that they had broken the glass and someone was inside somewhere. Archer ran halfway down the staircase when a figure emerged from behind a Henry Moore sculpture, a pistol in front of him. Archer saw his transplanted face on the head of Castor Troy. Instinctively, Archer used his height advantage, and, with toes pushing hard off the step's edge, he pounced on his enemy.

The two slammed together as the pistol went off, shattering the skylight. As broken glass rained down, Archer slugged Castor in the stomach, then the chin, making him tumble to the ground. The gun skipped away.

"Stay away from my family," Archer screamed. He pounced again, but Castor was ready. He rolled away quickly as Archer dived hard into the floor.

"Too late," Castor said as he sprang at Archer and locked a choking arm around his neck. "Your kid loves me. And your wife's an animal. Even I can't keep up with her." Castor eyed a jagged piece of glass—how good it would feel to slit his enemy's throat and feel the warm blood rush over his hand. Sean Archer was finally going to die. Before he did, however, Castor would sweeten his victory with an insult more cutting than the glass. He locked his arm tighter around Archer as he suffocated. Archer was incredulous when he felt Castor's tongue, hot and wet, caressing his ear like a lover's. "Tonight I'm going to bury my face in your wife's sweet pussy until she comes like Niagara Falls . . ." Castor said. Then he dropped his voice to a hiss and added, ". . . to celebrate your death."

It was the wrong thing to say. The glass nearly gouged Archer's throat when his entire being exploded with rage. His arm elbowed back into Castor, ramming him in the stomach and sending his lunch up like a projectile. Archer turned and heaved him into a pile of broken glass. Picking up the piece he'd been cut with, Archer turned his incandescent fury on Castor. Castor was stunned and disoriented, sure only that Archer was on the attack. Then a voice came from the end of the room.

"Sean! Where are you?"

It was Loomis, with his M-16 grenade launcher. He rushed in, saw "Castor," and fired. Archer leapt into an alcove whose door led to a stairwell that went to the rooftop. An alarm sounded when he pushed the door open. The grenade that Loomis had fired exploded and burst into flames on the shutting door.

"FUUUUUUUUCK!" Castor shouted, when he realized Archer had made it out. Castor ran to the burning staircase and, realizing he couldn't get through, ran through the rotunda and into the loft to get outside. Archer exited the stairwell and saw that the loft's rooftop was eerily empty as the SWAT agents swarmed below. He eyed a fire-escape railing, crawled to the building's ledge, and climbed down to the railing's platform—no one had seen him.

"Peekaboo, dumb fuck," said Pollux, squatting inside a window casing and smoking. Archer turned and found himself looking into the barrel of Pollux's pistol and was stunned. Archer's left hand jerked quickly against the gun just as Pollux squeezed the trigger. The bullet grazed Archer's arm, and he slipped and fell over the platform. His hands banged hard against the grating, but he managed to grasp the railing with his left hand and brought up his weak right. His hands ached and slipped till he was gripping only with fingertips.

"Remember me? Your baby brother?" Pollux taunted, and took the cigarette from his mouth. "Better put this out," he said, and dropped it into Archer's shirt. The shirt and his transplanted chest hairs were burning, stinging Archer's eyes. Pollux stomped on Archer's fingers and ground them as Archer screamed in pain.

Castor, his clothes covered in vomit, emerged with Loomis on the sidewalk below. Loomis yanked up his machine pistol and aimed it at Archer's dangling figure. Archer twisted and turned, anchored by Pollux's feet, and felt the fire escape shake loose from the wall—its rusty rivets were loosening from the bricks. In a flash, he sensed his one chance as Loomis took aim. "Wait for a better shot," Castor said.

Archer took that moment to plant his feet on the wall. Pollux aimed his gun at Archer's head and spit out his words. "You tricked me into telling you things I never told anyone. Now take them to your grave."

Archer pushed with the last bit of strength in his legs. The rivets creaked, then popped out as the fire escape pulled away. Pollux shifted and lost his balance. He grasped at the window casing and missed. The collapsing railing bent and dumped him far above the pavement.

As Pollux fell, Castor watched and felt the

world suddenly disintegrate. His brother pancaked with a sickening thud to the asphalt. In disbelief, Castor was suddenly blind and deaf, and he collapsed to the ground. He had momentarily blacked out, and when he came to, he vaguely saw Archer on the end of the bent staircase, arching through the window of a neighboring building. Castor couldn't concentrate on that, so absorbed was he with concern for his brother. Staggering to Pollux's draining body, Castor splashed through his brother's blood.

Pollux was slipping away fast. Castor desperately held him, telling him to hang on, hold tight. Loomis gulped and stared quietly until Castor saw him.

"Get a medic—now!" Castor shouted.

"Forget him, sir. It's only Pollux Troy."

Castor yielded to his first impulse. He jerked his gun up and fired into Loomis's forehead. As the body sank to the sidewalk, Castor felt no relief—his body was convulsing with rage. Drawn by the gunfire, Buzz and Wanda peered around the corner, then dropped their arms before approaching Castor.

"What happened?" Wanda asked, her forehead knitted in shock turning to grief as she saw Loomis's corpse.

"What the fuck do you think happened?" Castor screamed at her. "Castor Troy just shot him!"

Buzz and Wanda stared in disbelief. Castor's voice was a mix of rage and pathos when he commanded them. "What are you waiting for? Go! Go!" Once they had left, Castor turned to see if anyone was watching. Convinced he was alone, he buried his face in his brother's chest and felt its fading warmth. He saw Pollux's shoe lace was undone, and for the last time, he tied it.

"Sean Archer will pay, Pollux," he spoke to the corpse. "He'll pay with his family."

Archer raced to the abandoned building's rear and saw the rail yard through dust-covered windows. He found a window free of glass and, dangling from it, dropped from the second floor to the ground. Sprinting toward a maze of idle rail cars, he was buoyed with new hope as he distanced himself from the chaos, from the danger, from his powerful enemy. A freight train was approaching, faster than he liked, but he would have to try to jump on. As the train sped by, Archer ran in the same direction, and when a ladder appeared on a refrigerator car, he leapt on, took hold, and pulled himself up. He climbed to the car's top, lay on his back, and felt he might never get his breath back. He looked into the starless sky and didn't see any helicopters. The wind on his face felt cool and sweet. He half laughed, then half cried in relief.

Chapter 13

Castor did not go to Archer's home that dark, early morning. He went straight to the office. He sat rolling in the desk chair, staring out the window and drinking mescal laced coffee in clothes that stank from puke.

Lazarro had also come in early and was in his own office, packing boxes. In one of the boxes he had packed earlier were photocopies of Sean Archer's file he was secreting out; now he had come back for his own effects. He hoped to be done before nine, but soon realized he hadn't enough time or boxes to gather the relics of a career that spanned decades. He was making the third trip to his car when he passed Castor's dark doorway—he had yet to turn on the lights that morning.

Quietly, Lazarro stood with a box under his

arm, fascinated, as Castor had a sudden burst of rage. He stood at the bookshelf and smashed the glass to a framed photo of Eve and Jamie. He tore the picture into pieces, then crumpled the frame. He was about to hurl it when he noticed Lazarro standing there. *How long has he been watching?* Castor put on his impassive Archer face.

"What do you want?" Castor asked, his face slowly yielding to a sneer.

"Just wanted to wish you good luck . . . before I fade away." Lazarro's eyes squinted in suspicion. He had felt sure that "Archer" was on someone else's payroll, but now he entertained the notion that he had just gone crackers. "You deserve the job, Sean. You were right about the bomb. And right about where Castor would hide. Hell, you were even right about that stool pigeon Pollux."

Lazarro stepped into the office, set the box on the desk, and pierced Castor with his eyes. "You were only wrong about a few little things," he said, reaching to the floor and picking up pieces of the torn picture. He tucked them in his pocket, alarming Castor, who seated himself and rode the chair smoothly to the door. Before he closed it, he noticed Kim had arrived for work wearing a white leather minidress. "The suspense is killing me," he said, as he rose to shut the blinds between the offices.

"You start meeting with Brodie and Miller," Lazarro said, his eyes following Castor around the room. "Then they die when the Walsh clinic burns down. Your best friend is murdered, and you don't give a shit. Suddenly you're smoking, drinking, acting like a man with something to hide—"

How much does Lazarro suspect? Can he possibly know?

"I don't know who bought you, Sean, or what they're after. But retired or not, I'm going to find out."

Castor flipped on the light and the fluorescent tubes blinked on. He smirked, realizing Lazarro was still in the dark. "Victor, it's a pity that Washington couldn't find an emeritus position for a man with your keen eye. Okay, I do have a confession to make, but you aren't going to like it."

Castor sidled over to Lazarro and put a mock-friendly arm around his neck. "I'm Castor Troy," he said, whispering in Lazarro's ear.

"What? I . . . I don't understand."

With his free arm, Castor suddenly jabbed his fist into Lazarro's chest. He jabbed again. Lazarro's arms quivered at his side as he tried to raise them, but Castor kept jabbing. Gasping for breath and silently pleading for mercy, he looked in Castor's eyes and saw not a flicker of emotion. Castor was pounding now, harder and harder, at Lazarro's heart—until it finally seized up. Lazarro twitched in a death throe until his face and body went slack and he slumped to the ground. Castor lifted his wrist to search for a pulse and found none.

"Now you understand," he said, removing the pieces of photograph from Lazarro's pocket. He went to the desk and punched up the intercom. "Kim, cancel my ten o'clock," he said, and after a pause added, "Oh, and send for the paramedics. Victor Lazarro's having a heart attack." Castor looked in Victor's box, saw the Archer file, and stuffed it in his desk. He saw the mescal bottle. Hmmm.

All that coffee had him hyped up. He had time for a drink. He looked at his watch as the booze burned down his throat, then knelt beside Lazarro's body. The door flew open as two of the Bureau's paramedics rushed in. They found Castor vigorously pumping Lazarro's chest, applying CPR.

"Darn it, Victor, fight! Fight, gosh darn you!"

Castor banged his fist into Lazarro's chest as if from desperation—the paramedics would conclude this was how the sternum had been fractured. Castor turned a bedraggled face to them. They gently nudged him aside and tried to take the corpse's pulse. Castor tapped into his grief for Pollux and looked convincingly sad.

□ ■ □

After Archer leapt from the train, he rested. His body was a world-class collection of bruises, scrapes, fractures, and hematomas. But remembering that his family was endangered had him quickly back on the march. He had found a homeless man wearing an old fedora and some worn-out running shoes who was willing to trade them for Castor's pricey loafers. In the skies above, choppers were circling. In the streets below, squad cars prowled and commuters cursed at the FBI's roadblocks. Archer was absolutely certain they were all looking for him.

His plan to get home was only half-conceived when he began its execution. He appeared on Broadway in a part of town where the stores that catered to immigrant Latinos yielded to the tony outlets patronized by corporate executives at lunchtime. The passersby were used to seeing the homeless, but the most jaded of them stopped to gawk at Archer as he skirted a roadblock, picked up a trash can, and walked down the middle of the street in heavy traffic. Occasionally, he lowered the can to reveal his face which looked rubbery and wild-eyed. He was a man undone, spouting something like the Pledge of Allegiance at the top of his voice. "I pledge the legions to the slags of the United Arab Emirates . . . and to the pubble kins of Richard Stands one native under blood, ishkibibble, with liver and onions for Raul."

Cars screeched to a halt and honked as Archer crossed through heavy traffic to the sidewalk in front of an electronics store. He spun in a circle with the trash can. Pedestrians steered clear of the madness. When he was safely isolated, Archer heaved the can into the storefront window. It only cracked, so Archer picked up the can and screwed it back and forth through the fissure. He drove it through until the glass shattered.

The alarm blared and everyone on the street was watching. A few young opportunists in gangsta wear drew close to the window. Archer made a goofy face and danced the Swim as the youths made their selections and disappeared in the alleys. Clerks rushed out to battle more converging looters as an LAPD squad car hauled onto the curb. Everyone scattered but Archer. The cop riding shotgun jumped from the car and chased the last looter, who was running with a TV set.

Archer pulled the hat low over his face, flapped his lips, and repeated his pledge of legions to the Arab Emirates. The squad car's driver looked annoyed as he stood by his door, radio in hand, watching "the kook." Archer was almost crawling now, mooing like a cow, as he got close to the cop, who shooed him away.

Suddenly, Archer dived and yanked something from the cop's utility belt. Before the cop could react, Archer jumped up and sprayed his face with Comply-Gas. Gagging and sagging, the cop fell away from the door, and Archer slipped inside the car. No sooner had he landed his butt in the bucket seat than he hit the gas. He flipped a switch to the tinted windows, which darkened, obscuring him from the outside. The other cop returned without the looter, but with the broken television set, and watched the squad car tear away. As Archer drove, he realized that his daughter was right—it was easy to steal a police car.

In the FBI morgue, Castor averted his eyes as the attendant opened a slide drawer and pulled out a sheet-covered body.

"Get out," he said, and the attendant stared. The attendant had had a bad morning, with an alarm that didn't go off, a missed bus, and a coffee spill on his shirt. And now Sean Cocksucker was dissing him at a job where he made $6.50 an hour to keep a bunch of dead people on ice.

"Say what?"

"I said get out." Castor wouldn't look at him.

"You're one rude motherfucker," the attendant said. Castor thought about killing him—an easy gouge to the throat, and he could rip out his trachea—then decided against it.

"Leave or die!" he shouted, and the attendant had the sense to leave. He'd find out where this ass-eater had an office and leave something nasty to defrost in his file cabinet, something that would stink after a few days and have to be searched for. And then when he saw what part of the human body it was . . .

Alone with Pollux's body, Castor worked up to pulling the sheet away and looking at his brother's corpse. For the first time in his life, Castor genuinely questioned if there was an afterlife. If there was, he wanted to die and join Pollux, once he had finished with Archer. Closing his eyes, Castor could remember his brother as a sickly boy, with his hair in ringlets and a pale, yellow complexion like buttermilk. They were seven and five years old when their mother explained why she had given them names that the other kids made fun of. At school, they were called Castor Oil and Buttocks.

"Castor and Pollux were half brothers, and they loved each other so," she told them, handing them hot Kahlúa and cocoa at bedtime.

Castor remembered on that evening the ash from her Pall Mall had fallen into his mug.

"Pollux was the son of Zeus, who was the big cheese among the gods, a big feta cheese, since they were Greek gods. But Castor's father was a regular human, like your own dad. One day, Castor was killed for ripping off somebody's cows or something, and when Pollux found him dead, he nearly cried his eyes out. Castor was half-mortal, and had to go to Hades, the place of the dead. Pollux prayed to his daddy, Zeus, that he should die to join his brother in Hades. But Zeus wanted his son with him, so he let Pollux share his life with Castor. They spent half their time fartin' around up on Mount Olympus, and the other half hangin' in Hades. They were never separated again. Like you two never will be."

Castor had never imagined that would be untrue. He touched his brother's cold, colorless forehead before lovingly pulling the sheet over his face.

Squad cars and roadblocks seemed to be everywhere Archer drove. He had turned onto a minor thoroughfare and found more of them blocking both lanes to a main road where a traffic checkpoint had been installed. He took the first turn he could and found a quiet place to flip open the vehicle's porta-comp. He typed in his access code and registered a Priority Alert from Agent Sean Archer. Waiting and waiting, he despaired it wouldn't be accepted. He breathed a sigh of relief when he heard the dispatcher issue the command, a code zero-zero alert. Confusion ensued as all units were ordered haphazardly to proceed to all terminals east and west on the Metro Red Line. Castor Troy had been sighted entering the Parthenia Terminal and could emerge at any number of stations.

Archer looked in the rearview mirror and saw a rapid procession of squad cars splitting off east and west. Above him, the first of many choppers flew in the same directions. The TAC squads were piling into armored jeeps and following. Archer could head north in hopes that the armada of surveillance cars around his house had also roared away. He might soon be at home.

He parked the car a street over from his house and got out, lucky that no one was outside just then. He checked all the windows of the houses and found them empty of faces. Walking through a patch of ivy, he hoisted himself to his neighbors' cinder-block fence. He realized he had never seen these neighbors, but had only heard their voices and smelled their barbecues in summer.

Archer reached his own backyard. Hiding in the foliage of an avocado tree, he saw Lars in a lawn chair, tuning a police-band radio. Archer looked at the birdhouse, the one Jamie had made in Girl Scouts, and reached through the leaves to stick fingers inside the hole. He felt the key and dragged it out as a bluebird *caw-cawed* over his head. Lars looked up at the bird, but didn't see Archer's arm snapping back to the tree.

From the look on Wanda's face, Castor might have assumed he had walked into the bullpen with his own severed head under his arm. "What are you doing here?" she shrieked.

"Where should I be?" he asked, looking around and noticing it was as quiet as Christmas Day. "Where's everyone else?"

"Backing you up! Didn't you track Castor to the Parthenia Street Terminal?"

"What?"

"You radioed in your personal security code! Nobody knows that code but you."

The realization dawned on Castor in fresh waves of rage. Why hadn't he changed all the codes? Archer was much smarter than he had ever realized. "Obviously someone else knows it!" he screamed at Wanda. "Get everybody back to their posts—*now!*"

The old running shoes provided the benefit of silence as Archer tiptoed around his house. From outside the staircase, Archer saw Lunt's massive legs under the kitchen table. Between bites of cheese and crackers, Lunt was shaking the bullets from his pistol to clean it. When Lunt went for a coffee refill, Archer took the moment to steal up the stairs.

The door to the master bedroom was closed. He entered and saw that the bed hadn't been made. The shower was running. Archer saw Eve's nightgown on the bed, and a pair of Castor's black mesh bikini briefs on the floor. An angry flash ignited a chain reaction of fury, an explosion of indignation. Overwhelmed, he sat on the bed, lifted the nightgown, and smelled it. He was oblivious to the fact that the water had stopped and his wife would be entering the room. When she did, he had completely forgotten whose face he was wearing. "Eve," he murmured, as his body shook with sudden, terrifying sadness.

The look of horror on her face snapped him back to reality. She ran backwards into the bathroom, but Archer was on her, covering her mouth. She dropped her towel and kicked and scratched, but he managed to keep her mouth closed. As she bit into the calluses of his palm, he concentrated on his words.

"I'm not going to hurt you, Eve. Just don't scream, okay?"

He felt her teeth letting go. "Okay?" he pleaded. She nodded in his grip, and he eased off of her. He was stabbed by the utter look of fear on her face, of anger rising in her eyes. How much had he hurt this beautiful woman in the past?

"I know you," she gasped. "You're the one who called . . . you're Castor Troy. You killed my son."

Archer's eyes were watering, and she sensed his genuine pathos when he spoke to her. "I called. But I'm not Castor Troy. I'm your husband."

Eve was struggling again, but now in fear of someone who was obviously criminally insane. He tried to steady her as he spoke. "This time, you must listen. Last week, we were in bed . . . we had a fight after you touched my scar. I told you I had to go away."

She was startled by his possession of this intimate information. But her husband was in the FBI—perhaps their house was bugged and somehow this psychopath had heard them. "My assignment . . . Sean Archer's assignment, was to enter a federal prison as Castor Troy."

Eve suddenly calmed as she heard sirens coming toward the house. As the cops returned, she would play for time, keep him talking.

"How did he expect to do that?" she asked.

"An FBI surgeon gave me Castor's face. You knew of him, Malcolm Walsh, supposedly died in a fire. He handled the transplant, the vocal implant, everything. Somehow Castor came out of his coma and killed everyone who knew about the mission. But not before he was transformed into me."

Eve was stunned. The story was absurd—she was a surgeon and couldn't imagine that such a procedure was possible. And yet when she looked into the man's *brown* eyes, she saw something familiar, smelled someone she knew, heard the cadences of her husband in someone else's voice. From downstairs, Lars's voice boomed out.

"Dr. Archer, are you all right?"

She didn't know whether to answer him or scream for help. Archer made a shushing motion with his finger to his lips. "Listen," he whispered. "If you need hard evidence, get it. Your husband's blood type is O-negative. Castor's is AB."

Footsteps were clomping up the stairs. Eve opened her mouth to scream when Archer dropped to his knees and pleaded with her. "Don't, Eve. Remember the parachute dream? I'm falling, and I need your help."

"Dr. Archer, is everything okay?" Lars asked.

"I'm fine. I was just in the shower."

Archer almost smiled as he looked into his wife's eyes before jumping through the window and into a sycamore tree. Blood drained from her face as she looked at Castor's black briefs. Sean Archer wore boxers.

Eve sat in her study, unable to read, unable to pay bills, unable to do anything but shake even though it wasn't cold. She had closed her doors, so the Swedish monsters didn't know what she was doing. She was adding up the changes in her husband and feeling terrified as she recalled his strange behaviors: his cigarette breath, the beer bottles in his car, his evasiveness about the all-night dentist, the savage way he made love. She felt horribly alone with her secret but knew she must not go to the phone. When she heard the motor of her husband's Olds turning into the drive, she flipped on her computer and pretended to surf through the latest web sites on neurological disorders. Her heart was beating in her face when she heard Castor's voice in the living room.

"You two," he addressed Lunt and Lars. "Make your rounds. And tell those cops to stay off the lawn." Castor knocked sharply at her door, and she jumped.

"Come in."

She could barely turn to face him and feigned interest in a new sciatic procedure. "Hi," she said limply, as his hands dropped to her shoulders, and he felt her tension. Her muscles became even more rigid when he started massaging her.

"You're all in knots. Maybe another Date Night will help you relax."

"Not tonight," she said. She placed a cold hand on his own to stop him. "I'm way behind in my Continuing Ed."

Castor studied her, sensed her fear, and wondered what she guessed, what she knew. He took a firm hold of her shoulders. "You think I've been acting strange. Like a completely different person."

Eve hesitated, gave the slightest nod of her head.

"Okay. I have a confession to make. But you aren't going to like it."

Castor's fingers slowly collapsed around her slender neck. "I read your diary," he said. "I've been trying to change. Trying to be more like the man you want me to be."

Eve held her breath. As she exhaled, she realized there was a logic to it all. Of course this man was her husband. She started to relax and enjoyed the warm weight of his hands on her shoulders.

"And to prove it," he said, starting the massage again, "I'm taking you and Jamie away on a trip. Right after the memorial service."

Eve's heart fluttered. So many of Sean's colleagues had died lately.

"What memorial service?"

"Victor Lazarro had a heart seizure . . . right in my office. It was horrible."

"Oh my, God. Sean . . ." Eve rose to comfort him and looked in his eyes. Castor poured it on. He gave the performance of a man whose immense grief could not be held back by his usual capacity for stoic reserve.

"First Tito. Now Victor," he said, with a cry in his voice. Holding her tight, he topped it off with, "Please don't tell me I'm going to lose you, too . . ."

"Of course not," Eve replied, and returned his embrace. But as he was stroking her back and holding back his sobs, she was wondering if she had a lancet in her medical bag.

□ ■ □

Eve had feared getting in bed, but knew she would trigger the suspicions of the man who might not be her husband if she didn't turn in when he did. She had fended off his advances by telling him she had discovered a yeast infection. That was something he didn't want to get up his urethra again, did he? She realized she had read the same page in her book for the tenth time as Castor slumbered fitfully. Finally he had turned on his side away from her. She turned to the back of the book, picked up a lancet, and stuck him. He woke with a start as she dropped the lancet into an opened box of candy.

"What was that?" he asked.

"What was what?" she responded, turning the page and popping a cherry cordial in her mouth.

"Something bit me," he said, rubbing his shoulder blade.

Eve rubbed his shoulder for him. "Probably a mosquito," she said, getting out of bed. "I'll close the window." She shut the window and turned out the light. After Castor had gone back to sleep, she left the bed and took the lancet to the downstairs bathroom, where her clothes were hanging. She squeezed the lancet, and the smallest drop of blood fell into a glass vial. After quietly dressing, she left the house for her car.

Eve was unlocking the Volvo, her head throbbing in fear, when a hand grabbed her. She stifled a scream and turned to see the policemen posted to guard her.

"Sorry, Dr. Archer," said Officer Derner. "Where are you going at this hour?"

"An emergency," she said. "An emergency at the hospital. Excuse me."

"Sorry, ma'am, but one of us will have to escort you."

"Fine," she said, and Derner opened her door for her. The other cop was walking back to his squad car when Eve shook him by the sleeve. "Please don't wake my husband. He's exhausted." The cop nodded.

Outside her office, the bored cop leaned against the wall. The vast white corridors were empty except for a cleaning man chasing dust with a mop. Inside, Eve paced anxiously as the blood analyzer clicked away. "Please be O-neg. Please," she muttered as the machine made its final click. The monitor read: MALE * TYPE AB. She stared at the monitor, frozen, unable to assimilate the information. For a moment, she was confused. Was it her husband, or Castor Troy who was O-negative? Her mind was a tornado of confusion, and she was terrified and sickened at sudden memories of sex with someone who couldn't have been her man, a man who had had her seven different ways.

"Oh, God, Sean," she cried, burying her face in her hands and collapsing in her desk chair.

"Thanks for believing me," said a voice. Eve turned to see Archer emerging from behind the darkness of an X-ray screen. She reached for her opened purse and pulled out a pistol. With calm authority, she pivoted and aimed toward her husband.

"What are you doing? Where did you get that gun?" he asked.

"I took it from my pseudo-husband."

"Why point it at me? I'm the real thing."

"I don't know that," she said, and felt a weird exasperation. She had been pulled through the Looking Glass and didn't know what to expect. "Maybe the real Sean Archer is dead."

He rolled his eyes while shaking his head. The gesture looked familiar to Eve. She aimed the gun at his face and commanded him. "Tell me . . . tell me about the all-night dentist."

Archer went to lean against the counter, but she jerked the gun at him. He stood his place and raised his hands above his head. Eve searched his brown eyes as he spoke.

"Eighteen years ago, I took a date out for

chicken and ribs, not knowing she was a strict vegetarian. No animal products of any kind—milk, eggs, even gelatin. The only thing she would eat was the three bean salad. When the night couldn't get any worse, she broke her eye-tooth on a pebble in the salad. She was wearing pigtails and overalls with a gingham shirt, and the broken tooth made her look like a hillbilly. I bought some Black Jack gum and used it to black out my own teeth so she would feel better. In the car, we listened to the country-music station. Somehow she and I had fun driving around that evening, laughing and looking for an all-night dentist."

Eve's arm was dropping. With her free hand she wiped at tears. Archer knelt before her, looked in her tear-stained face and finished the story. "And even though it must have hurt . . . you still kissed me."

She was wailing now. The gun dropped, and she smacked his shoulder. "Christ, Sean! How could you put us in this position? Do you know . . . do you know what he did to me?"

He winced and put his hand on her thigh. "Whatever happened, whatever he did, I know it's my fault. I know I can never make it up to you."

"But you're damn sure going to try," she said through sniffles. "In the meantime, how are we going to get you out of this?" She was pulling herself together.

Archer did something he needed to do. He hugged his wife, a full embrace, and their bodies burned against each other. He couldn't bring himself to kiss her though . . . not with Castor Troy's lips.

At the same moment, Castor jumped when he woke from a fitful sleep and realized Eve was gone from the bed. He pulled off his T-shirt, flipped on the bathroom light, and examined his shoulder in the mirror. He rubbed the red spot and did not see the bump of a mosquito bite, but a tiny V-shaped puncture.

Chapter 14

Eve sifted through her supply cabinet and showed Archer a yellow vial of Ketalar. "This will knock him out for hours," she said.

"Good. What's his schedule for tomorrow?"

"He doesn't tell me any more than you ever did. All I know is, after Victor's memorial service, he's taking Jamie and me away." Archer recolied "Victor's dead?" He struggle to blot out his culpability in Lazarro's death, just as he had to with Tito's: that reckoning would come later. He also realized that when Eve and Jamie went away, they wouldn't be coming back.

"Where's the service?" he asked.

"Saint Mary's-by-the-Sea."

His son's burial place. Archer shook his head, the irony not lost on him. It was all coming 'round on the Wheel. He realized that for him, Saint Mary's had its advantages.

"It's good, Eve. Up there I'll have plenty of cover. It's a tough place to secure. I'll have a chance."

"What will you do?"

Eve looked in her husband's eyes behind the living mask as he formulated his plan. "I'll hit him with a trank dart. Once he's unconscious, I'll try to get to Buzz and Wanda before the security team gets to me."

"What can I do?" she asked, loathing the idea that she could only stand by, like some helpless female in an old-time movie.

"Leave town," he said. "Think up a good excuse. I don't want you or Jamie anywhere near that service."

She shook her head. "No. I can cover for Jamie, but if I'm not there, he'll suspect something."

Archer wasn't sure.

"The second you make your move," she said, "all hell is going to break loose. If I'm there beside him, I can take charge. I'm *his* wife, remember?"

Archer was reconsidering. She gently smirked at him, and said, "There's no way around it. For once, you *need* me."

His eyes were welling. He looked down at the

floor, then at her. "I've always needed you," he said, and reached for her again. Her hands were running up and down his back as a current of warmth cycled between them.

"Sean, what are the odds?" she asked, her deep worry evident in her brow.

"Terrible. But it's the best we can do with what we have." He broke away and locked her eyes. "If it doesn't happen, take Jamie and don't look back."

"It'll happen," Eve said, and fell back in his embrace. He jolted, suddenly aware of the fast-approaching footsteps.

"Do doctors travel in packs?" he asked.

"Only when we're golfing."

"It's him," Archer said. "I know it."

"This way," she commanded, and Archer ran with her. They exited through a door that led to a sitz bath that connected to the main corridor. From there, they could turn into the burn ward.

Castor and the Swedes rushed into her office, guns leveled. Seeing it was empty, they turned back into the corridor. They proceeded to the burn ward and saw Eve wrapping gauze on the face of a "crispy critter." When she saw them and their guns, she gave out with a short scream, then clutched her chest. "Sean! What are you doing here?"

"That's what you're going to explain to me," said Castor.

"Didn't the police tell you? This is an emergency!"

Eve continued wrapping the gauze when Lars yanked it from her. Lunt tore away at the bandages.

"What are you doing?" she shouted. "Sean, make them stop. Mr. Alandro is *very ill*."

"Not as ill as he's going to be," said Castor, as Lunt pulled away enough gauze to reveal the hideously fresh burns of the victim. His eyelids were completely gone, and his exposed eyeballs shifted in pain under the harsh ceiling light. Eve was red with anger, and Castor was white with panic as he was reminded of his own faceless moments in Walsh's complex. He turned away. The Swedes were both fascinated and repulsed. Eve grabbed the gauze from Lars and rewrapped Alandro.

"I'm sorry," Castor said. "But what's a guy to think when his wife runs off in the middle of the night?"

Eve looked at him like he was just the cutest and kissed him on the mouth. "It's my fault. I should've woken you before I left. Now please . . . let me get back to work. Who did you think was under these bandages? My lover?"

"Well . . . yeah," he answered. Eve rolled her eyes. After Castor and the boys left, she wiped his ugly taste from her mouth. Archer emerged from the room's bathroom and hugged his wife. "Be strong," he said, and she nodded.

"My God, I love you," she said, and buried her face in his chest. Sean could barely tear himself away.

Castor wasn't taking any chances. He marched quietly back to his car as the Swedes hustled to keep pace. "Stay here," Castor ordered. "And watch her like a hawk."

"Think she knows?" Lars asked.

"Doesn't matter," Castor answered. "She's going to be dead by tonight anyway. They're all going to be dead. The wife, the kid . . . the father."

Archer left the hospital the same way he had come in, through the garbage chute. He slid into a Dumpster and emerged, knowing he needed funeral clothes and a weapon, preferably a sniper rifle. Dietrich's "safe house" in Topanga Canyon was a long way off as Archer remembered—he knew its general vicinity and recalled it was up the road from a Hindu temple. As he passed through a poor Latino neighborhood, he eyed an old Ford pickup from the late fifties. On the side, fading letters read GONZALEZ AND SONS. It was a gardener's truck, and, in a couple of hours, the Gonzalez family would be starting to load it with the equipment of their trade. The hood was banged up and easy to open. Archer hot-wired the pickup with a clothes hanger he found in some trash. He promised himself that Mr. Gonzalez would be repaid for his sacrifice that day. *Hell, I'll hire them to do my own yard.*

The truck rumbled over a gravel road to Hassler's ranch house deep in the canyon. The noise woke Sasha, who slept lightly since the attack on the loft. She had stayed hidden inside the compartment with her son, keeping him quiet for seven hours until the police had gone. Thinking they were coming for her now, she was relieved to see it was "Castor" getting out of the old Ford. She ran down the stairs in her nightie to let him in.

"Caz, you're a goddamned cat," she said. "Though I suspect you're running out of lives."

"Got any coffee?" he asked. She nodded, and he followed her to the kitchen.

"Did your brother make it?" he asked. A long silence passed. She shook her head grimly.

"Aldo's dead, too," she said.

Archer was unmoved by the deaths of the men, but was wounded by her pain and allowed a respectful silence.

"How's the boy?" he asked, as she dumped coffee in the maker.

"He wasn't breathing too well for a while. He was out playing yesterday." She took a moment, then looked at Archer. "Thank you," she said.

"For what?"

"Saving his life." Archer gave her a slight nod.

"I need a sniper rifle," he said. "And some clothes. A dark suit. Is that okay?"

"I knew you didn't come to see me," she answered, and disappeared. As the coffee dripped, Archer ate some green bananas and snacked from the refrigerator. He looked in the living room and saw she was working on a painting of Adam. She was talented, he thought, and Eve would like her work. Sasha came back with a long case, some ammo, and the clothes. He told her of his plan to shoot "Archer" at the funeral.

"Look, Caz," she said, as Archer dressed in front of her. "There's gonna be FBI agents all over that place. Maybe you should have some backup. We could make some calls. There's plenty of us left who want Sean Archer. It's because of him my brother is dead." Her face darkened.

"Us? No, Sasha," he said, zipping up the pants. "Believe me, this isn't your fight."

He picked up the rifle and turned to leave. Her arms were folded, and in her eyes was a vortex of emotions. Archer felt he had made a mistake in looking at her face—she was so lovely, so fragile, so tragic in her attraction to Castor. He went to kiss her, not passionately, but nobly.

"For whatever it's worth, whatever happens today, I can promise you that Sean Archer will be off your back forever," he said after kissing her. Before he went out the door, he turned and said, "Thanks, Sasha."

She wondered about him as he jumped in the truck. When had he gotten manners?

Should she wear black? In Los Angeles in the last decade of the millennium the tradition of wearing black to funerals was almost considered quaint. People wore pretty much what they wanted to, and one was as likely to see black at weddings as at funerals. She realized what she was really trying to do was distract herself from this fateful morning's impending events. Yes, she would wear black to honor Victor Lazarro, as a sign of her mourning. He had been a good man, a gentleman, and her husband's friend and mentor. She knew his wife would appreciate the sentiment.

That decided, her mind turned once more to how she could help save her husband's life. It would demand a performance worthy of a great actress, and she knew she was visibly nervous. She remembered back to her high-school drama lessons and her coach telling her to take her negative feelings and "use them." The first act of today's drama would be easy, dealing with her daughter once Castor had left the house. It was a bit more difficult than she anticipated since Jamie *wanted* to attend the funeral. Eve insisted it was better she go to school and was forced to make a financial arrangement. Moments later, Eve put on her sunglasses as she approached Castor waiting in the limo.

"Where's Jamie?" he asked.

"That's what I'd like to know. She stole fifty dollars from my purse and took off. You know how difficult it is getting her into a proper dress."

Castor's eyes narrowed as he tried to read her. He could only vaguely see her eyes from behind the sunglasses.

"I'll deal with her later," he said.

"Good. Because I am fed up," said Eve, mildly shaking her head. She placed her purse on her lap, looking as proper as she had the first time Castor accompanied her to St. Mary's. With her face forward, she looked at the side of his head and noticed he had tucked in the receiver of his earphone. He seemed to be getting a message on it now.

Rain was not falling on Victor Lazarro's

funeral. It was a postcard-perfect Los Angeles day, with a sky as blue as a movie star's swimming pool and clouds as white as cosmetic cotton puffs. The beautiful, rolling bluffs above the ocean were tufted in wet, green grass where jackrabbits feasted and felt safe. Even the sun-drenched tombstones had a strange cheeriness, as if they were charmingly fake, plucked from a Hollywood set. Rows of white chairs were set up at the bottom of the cemetery knoll. As Eve expected, few of the mourners were dressed in black, and some were downright colorful. The brilliant flowers behind the casket added to the garish cheer. Only the mourners' faces were dark. Several of them, like Eve, wished it would rain to gloom things down.

Every fifteen seconds she fought the urge to look over her shoulder for Sean, knowing it would rouse Castor's suspicions. When she first stepped from the limo, she took a surreptitious glance around, but hadn't Lars and Lunt been watching her in that moment? She took a sideways glance at them from behind her glasses. Yes, they were glued to her.

Castor lead Eve to the front row as the ceremony began. The Lazarros' grown children eyed Castor with contempt and openly whispered about "Archer." It pained Eve when Renata Lazarro would not meet her gaze. Eve could only figure Castor had done something as "Archer" that offended her husband before he died. In the back of Eve, Buzz and Wanda had arrived. Buzz had asked Wanda to go with him, as a prelude to a real date, and though the occasion was a dark one, they had the glow of a mutually attracted couple.

The priest was a handsome young Mexican-American with a perfect peanut-butter complexion and the kind of thick black hair that sent bald men into paroxysms of envy. Though his cassock was black, he wore a sash with bands of bright serape colors. His presence was one more cheerful addition until he mustered the solemnity of the occasion with a mastery beyond his years. His voice was a somber singsong as he addressed the bereaved.

"We are here to celebrate the life of Victor Lazarro. We all knew him as a man who dedicated his life to defending the peace and prosperity this nation so richly enjoys . . ."

"Hallelujah, brother!" Castor shouted. Eve turned red with embarrassment as the other agents smirked and elbowed each other. Buzz and Wanda exchanged looks of amused puzzlement. Castor realized the Lazarro family was staring at him and that he must have committed some *faux pas.* The priest glanced briefly at him, then continued.

". . . but not all of you know what a deeply spiritual man Victor was. It was his wish that his requiem be performed in Latin. *In Nomine Patris et Filii et Spiritus Sancti.*"

The priest crossed himself, a signal to other Catholics to do the same. Eve almost smirked as she watched Castor make something which looked like an air swastika.

Archer could have knelt behind any number of headstones, and some of them might have given him a better vantage point. But he was drawn to that of Michael Noah Archer, Beloved Son and Brother. He brushed away the toys Eve had left while he was in Erewhon and checked his assemblage of the rifle. He inserted the trank dart's tip in the sedative and pulled the latch, watching the yellow Ketalar fill the glass casing.

"Domine, de morte aeterna in die illa tremenda quando caeli movendi sunt et terra," the priest intoned, as Eve took a discreet glance at her watch. She had a sudden sympathy for her husband she had never had before—if this was the kind of tension he had to live with on a daily basis, it would have worn her down as well, made her colder than she had ever imagined. Castor was keeping one eye glued to her and saw that her mind had wandered off.

Archer was an excellent marksman, but he trembled when he thought, once again, that he only had one shot. He kissed the dart, chambered it, then twisted a knob on the range finder. He peered carefully over the headstone and found Castor's head. For a moment Archer reeled and had a sense of déjà vu. No, he hadn't been here before, but the Wheel had come full circle: Archer was the sniper, and Castor was the target. This time, there would be no unintended casualty.

"*Requiem aeternum dona eis, Domine . . . Amen,*" the priest finished. Eve realized that if she weren't so preoccupied, she would have been deeply moved by the priest's words. He had all the fresh piety and fervor of someone who had recently left the seminary. Young women among the pews mourned the priest's decision to choose God over one of them.

Sean Archer was in the grips of his own religious experience. The growing feeling he had was more than a premonition, it was a certainty. It was the same indisputable assurance felt by a baseball player who knows he will get a home run, the confidence a professional gambler heeds when he must go to the track, the unshakable faith of an actress who has no doubt her audition will land her the lead. The moment was now. His finger was squeezing.

And then he had to stop.

A figure crossed in front of Castor, blocking

Archer's shot. Her hair tumbled away from her face, and Archer nearly collapsed when he saw it was Jamie.

She squeezed in between Castor and her mother. Eve could only stiffen as her daughter slipped her a fifty-dollar bill. "Thanks anyway, Mom. But I wanted to be here for you . . . and Dad." Castor smirked and stared into Eve's eyes. *I know you know,* his expression said to her, and her fear rose to a new level.

Jamie could not read the expression on their faces. To her mother, she seemed to have done something awful. And her "father" looked as if his worst suspicions had been confirmed. Neither of them said anything, and he took Jamie's hand and intertwined his fingers with hers.

The Bureau's honor guard stepped forward, shouldering their rifles and commencing their gun salute. Archer wondered if his moment had passed, then fought off his doubts as superstition. He steadied himself and reaimed the rifle. The calm of his premonition returned—he would make his target. Castor was dead center in the scope.

Archer was squeezing the trigger when he heard the thud of boots running in the grass behind him. What was that? His hands barely trembled as the trank dart exploded silently from the barrel of the rifle.

Eve shut her eyes when she felt the vague gust of a projectile and prayed it wasn't Sean's dart. She suddenly panicked, sure that it was. The dart had gone just wide of Castor's neck and had sunk in the grass, its short voyage obscured by the din of the honor guard's salute.

As the blanks fired, Archer knew he had to turn, to run and do battle. But it was too late. The heavy butt of an automatic pistol had cracked against his head and stunned him. It came down a second time on his fifth vertebrae. He was falling, falling down, and deep into that endless hole to the Little Death. His last realization was that the pistol's silenced barrel was in his ear. The Big Death was looming before him like a black sun of boiling tar ready to suck him in.

The honor guard wrapped the flag from the coffin and presented it to Mrs. Lazarro. Eve had to look around now, sure it had all gone wrong. Castor was touching the earphone, getting a message, an important message. He attached the rest of the headset and wandered off from her, turning his back.

"Lunt. Take Jamie, bring the car around, then meet me in back of the sanctuary," he said realizing that, in Pollux's absence, he had finally distinguished one twin from the other. Then he turned to stare at Eve.

The mourners were quietly chatting, meeting and greeting as they ambled to their cars. On a panicky impulse, Eve took the momentary opportunity presented to approach Wanda and Buzz.

"Wanda!" Eve cried out. Wanda heard the desperation in Eve's voice, turned to her and read her face.

"Eve. What's wrong?"

Eve clutched Wanda's arm, then saw Lunt by the limo, staring at them. He was tightening his "friendly" grip around Jamie.

"I'll . . . I'll call you," Eve said, defeated. Castor joined her.

"Excuse us," Castor said, leading her away. "We're going inside to light a candle for the dearly departed."

Buzz and Wanda looked at the "Archers" heading to the church, and then looked at each other. Something was wrong. Were they arguing?

The church was dim. A few tiny flames flickered in votive candles. Eve's heart sank when she saw that the pews were empty. Castor was hustling her past the altar and into the sacristy, where he slammed the door behind them. She saw Lunt's back first, then through his legs she saw her husband. He was deathly still. She gasped and searched for any movement, hoping she had seen the shallow rise of his chest.

"Look who we caught creeping around. Castor Troy," said Castor.

Eve was ill. Feverish and overcome with nausea, her legs turned to water. "Why is he here?" she asked.

"Before I turn him in, I thought we'd pay him back for everything he's put us through." As Castor finished his words, he kicked Archer hard in the rib cage, then slammed his foot in his gut. "Come on, baby. Join the fun," he said, kicking Archer over and over.

"You fucking sadist!" she screamed, and charged Castor.

"Eve. Such language, from you of all people," he said, and easily subdued her. "Too bad. Part of me was hoping you didn't know. Guess which part?"

He threw her on the floor, and she clung to her husband. His body was still warm. She could hear his heart beat when she pressed her ear to his chest. "Eve," Archer said, and she saw him open his eyes. One of them was puffed and swollen. Though it hurt him to raise his arm over his bruised ribs, he tried to hold her as she wept. Castor snickered.

"Isn't that cute," he said, and circled them. "Did you really think it would be that easy, you dumb fuck?" Castor kicked Archer's ear, and resumed his rant. "The boys wanted to just kill you and make your body disappear. But I had a better plan. One that would tie up all the loose ends."

Castor lit a cigarette. Archer's kicked ear was ringing. "Here I am, attending the funeral of my mentor, when something goes terribly wrong. Eluding security, Castor Troy—that's you Sean," he said, flicking ashes on Archer's face, "Castor Troy attacks. I kill you. But too late. You've already murdered my beloved wife and daughter. And the last three people who could expose me are dead."

Archer looked up at him. "Leave them out of this," he muttered. "This is between you and me."

Castor paused and sucked on his smoke. "It *was* between you and me. Even your little boy. That wasn't supposed to happen, Sean. But *you* couldn't let it go."

"No father could," Archer whispered.

Castor snarled. "Appealing to my sense of family won't work, Sean. I thought you knew me better than that."

Archer was casting about for some hope. Nothing occurred to him until he realized his foot was next to a heavy wrought-iron candle-stand. He snaked his foot under its short legs. It wasn't much of a chance, but he had to try. If he could get it to fall, he could pick it up and use it as a weapon, maybe bash in Castor's skull.

"I know some things that even you don't know, *Caz,*" Archer said, and Castor winced. Had Archer been doing Sasha? No. He was a wimp, the type who left his dick at home with wifey. "You have a son," Archer said. "I've met him. His name is Adam."

"I imagine I've got a dozen kids—so what?" Castor growled, cocking his pistol and utterly indifferent. "No more head games. First your wife dies. Then your daughter. Then you." The pistol went down toward Eve's head. Archer went to jerk the candlestand down when someone knocked at the door. Castor looked at Lunt, who shrugged.

"It's Lars, with the kid," Castor said. "Bring her in. Just one big happy family." Lunt went to the door and opened it. He backpedaled, with his hands over his head. It was Sasha. She entered with a Kalishnikov machine gun. She wanted to kill the Swedish "traitors."

"Sasha!" Castor gasped in disbelief. She saw the gun off to the side in his hand. Sasha had the clear advantage.

"That's Ms. Hassler to you, Archer. Drop it."

"Sasha, I . . ."

"I said *drop it!*" Sasha screeched. Castor complied. Eve broke away from Archer. At the same moment, Lars and Jamie pulled up in the car outside the church. Over his headset, Lars could hear that something was wrong.

Sasha fell to Archer's side, with her weapon firmly pointed at Castor. "Are you okay, Caz?" she asked. Archer nodded.

"You're making a mistake!" Castor shouted. "I'm Castor, he's Archer. Sasha—baby—just give me a minute to explain!"

Sasha sneered. "Your jokes are just killing me. Let me return the favor." She was squeezing the trigger when Lars charged in, shooting bullets at the ceiling. *What the fuck is going on?*

"Shoot, Lars!" Castor shouted.

"Who?"

"All of them!"

In the brief moment Lars hesitated, Archer kicked at the legs of the candlestand, and it fell across his chest. Castor dived for his gun, and Sasha fired at Lars. Lunt fired into Sasha as Eve kicked Castor in the balls. Archer rose with the stand and smashed its iron base into Lunt's head. His bullets fired into Sasha's shoulder. As she squeezed the trigger, the gun veered and its bullets riddled Lunt, whose body slumped into their path. Sasha dropped the Kalishnikov, and Archer went for it. Castor fled under Lars's cover. Castor needed to get to the Feds, who he would order to gun down "Castor Troy."

"Find Jamie and get help!" Archer shouted at Eve. Dazed and confused, Archer limped out to the sanctuary. He fired at Lars and Castor, who were firing back as they tried to make it out the entrance. Eve crawled under the fusillade and exited through an emergency side door. She ran to the parking lot and was breathless when she reached the car.

"Jamie?" she cried out. "Jamie!"

The car was empty. Wanda and Buzz were getting in their car and noticed her. Eve looked back at the church as bullets shredded the stained-glass windows. "What the fuck?" Buzz shouted, and they ran to Eve.

"Where's Sean?" Wanda asked.

Eve was panicked, breathing hard. "Wanda, I've got to tell you something. Something crazy."

Sasha was in agony. But she saw Castor's pistol on the floor and went to it. She had never shot a gun with her left hand, but she would have to try. She staggered from the sacristy and saw Archer barricaded behind the front pew. Each time Castor and Lars tried for the door, Archer opened fire, and they ducked back behind the last pew.

"Get down," Archer screamed at Sasha as Lars emerged, firing from the side of the pew.

"Gimme a piece," Castor commanded Lars, and he threw his boss the pistol in his ankle holster. Sasha would not get down, and fired at Lars, missing him as he unleashed his fire. Then Castor popped up. Archer tried to yank Sasha to the floor as Castor aimed, but the bullet caught her in the neck, and she dropped. Archer knew from the gushing blood that the rupture was fatal. She fell to the ground and turned her warm, poignant eyes on him as the floor soaked with blood. The red pool of liquid framed and contrasted her whitening face.

"Help Adam," she managed to get out. "Don't let him . . . end up like us . . ."

Archer took a moment to stroke her face. He looked in her eyes and said, "I will." Her long-lashed lids blinked slowly, then stilled. In a brief moment of silence, Archer was gritting his teeth. How sadly fitting that it was Castor who had killed this woman.

The short quiet was interrupted by Lars, who fired into the altar. His bullets caught the cables of the crucifix and it fell forward. Castor was up and watching. Archer jumped out of the way of the crucifix as it smashed the pew into pieces.

Castor and Lars took the moment's respite to run. Archer jumped up just in time to aim at Lars. The first bullet shot his ear off. The second one snapped his spinal cord from the neck down. Lars tumbled, unable to move any part of his body as Archer sprinted past. Lars's brain was still active, but his lungs were no longer working. Alive long enough to observe his own suffocation, he wanted to scream and couldn't. His boss had forgotten him and retreated to the mazelike hedges of the church's formal gardens.

Archer emerged in the plant- and statue-filled maze. The lower leaves of a hedge shook, and Archer aimed and squeezed the trigger. It was just a rabbit, but the gun failed to fire—he checked the clip and saw that it was empty. "Shit," he muttered, and threw the gun in the dirt. In the distance, he saw Castor moving stealthily through the narrow paths. Weak though he was, Archer was steadily drawing nearer to Castor, who couldn't maintain his pace. He was winded and choking on coughed-up phlegm, the result of years of smoking.

Archer kept gaining on him. Castor looked over his shoulder. He would not be caught from behind. He stopped, turned to aim the gun, and saw that Archer had vanished. Where was he? Archer suddenly leapt over a hedge and pounced, the impact knocking the gun from Castor's hand. The men crashed hard, a dervish of flesh and venom as they sputtered into a clearing. Each was brutally strangling the other, their fingers gouging deep into each other's throats. Archer felt blood racing down the back of his esophagus and something jerk in his trachea.

"Give up, Castor. People are going to find

out," he croaked. The larynx adapter had been dislodged. His voice echoed with garbled, robotic static.

"Not if I kill you first," Castor said, pulling his knees onto Archer's chest and using them to break his grip. They scrambled for the gun. Castor was within reach of it when suddenly a hand from between the juniper bushes picked it up and aimed it at both of them.

Jamie. Archer and Castor froze, panting heavily, as they stared at the girl's frightened face.

Chapter 15

"Give it here, Jamie," Castor said.

"No, Jamie. Don't do it!" Archer shouted. He realized he no longer had Castor's voice, that his own was back. Jamie gawked. "That's right, Jamie. Listen to my voice. I'm your father."

"It's a trick," Castor shouted. "*I'm* your father."

Baffled, Jamie swung the gun back and forth. She considered that Castor might not be her father. Flashes of recent memories about him didn't fit, but how could her father possibly look like this other man?

"Shoot him, Jamie," Castor shouted.

"No, honey, don't . . ." Archer pleaded.

"Shoot him!"

Jamie's arm swung slowly toward her real father. She fired. She was startled by the bang and thrown by the recoil. Archer reeled as the slug grazed his shoulder. Castor bounded up, grimaced, and snatched the gun from her. "You idiot. No kid of mine would miss so badly." He backhanded her face with a hard smack, and she stumbled to a tree.

Castor aimed at Archer's head. "For Christ's sake, Sean. Let's end this fucking thing, okay?"

Castor squeezed the trigger and Archer closed his eyes. A shot rang out, but Archer was still alive. Who had fired?

"Hold it!" said a female voice. Wanda and Buzz had burst into the clearing, their guns leveled. Eve and other agents were right behind them. Castor sighed, and said, "Just saving the taxpayers the cost of a trial. So everyone take a hike."

Wanda shook her head. "No. You're both under arrest until a DNA test proves who's who."

"I'm *ordering* you to back off!" Castor roared. Several agents wavered, but Wanda was almost convinced of Eve's claim.

"Put—it—down," Wanda commanded.

Jamie was rising as Castor shrugged and made a face as goofy as Gomer Pyle. "Can't blame me for trying," he said, and the agents were diverted by his show as he flailed his arms and mugged. In a swift movement, his face turned to pure rage as he leapt at Jamie, jerked her under him by her chin, and stuck the gun in her cheek. Eve gasped. Archer, reenergized, struggled to his feet. Castor used Jamie as a shield and backed out of the clearing to a gate. She couldn't talk—her teeth were biting her tongue.

"Say good-bye to father figure," Castor said, using his butt to push open the gate. She allowed him to drag her, her heels scraping in the dirt, as she reached under her dress. Castor was jerking her through the gate when she whipped out the switchblade and uncovered it with a quick flip of her wrist. She jabbed it deep into his thigh and twisted, just as he had taught her. As he howled and wrenched it from his thigh, she dived away. "You ungrateful delinquent!" he shouted, as the agents opened fire. He ran haltingly to the path in a cluster of pines that led to the bluff's edge.

Castor had reached the pines when a confused security agent stepped into the path, an Uzi in his arms. He looked at Castor's face. "Agent Archer?" he asked. Castor answered by plugging him and taking his Uzi. Just beyond the pines were the bluffs, and beyond them, the promise of the Pacific.

Eve was looking over her daughter, making sure she was all right. "She's okay," she said to Archer, who took that as his cue.

Archer walked toward Wanda, who still had her gun trained on him. "Stand back!" she shouted, but Archer, exasperated, kept walking toward her. "I need your piece," he said. "Come on, Wanda. It's me, your boss who's got a stick up his ass."

Wanda froze, but then her finger was squeezing. Archer jumped at her, deflected the bullet, then grabbed the gun. He rushed to the garden gate, experiencing a kind of tunnel blindness. Castor had become Archer's sole focus again as he sighted the limping figure at the bluff's edge. Castor looked out over the marina at sunbathers and yachts before skidding down the bluff over the rough, scrub-covered surface. His ears were tuned to revving motors, and he went in their direction. Archer reached the top of the bluff and looked down to see Castor hobbling along a pier to a boat slip. Two relaxed and suntanned crews were tuning up their cigarette boats, laughing, and egging each other on before a race.

The first boat's captain looked at Castor's twisted, bleeding figure and was concerned for him. Castor saw his compassion and exaggerated the wounded look on his face.

"Hey, are you all right?" the captain asked.

"No," Castor answered, painfully clutching at the lump in his jacket. He whipped out the

Uzi and shot the captain dead. The rest of the crews fell away screaming as Castor jumped in a boat and throttled it up. The boat started out toward the open sea, then jerked back—it was anchored.

"Cut it loose," Castor shouted, waving the Uzi. "Cut it loose or you all die!" he shouted at them. No one moved.

"You! Do it!" he screamed at a woman closest to the rope's end. She nervously tugged up the anchor, then threw it in the boat. Castor was tearing off when Archer reached the pier and the adjoining cigarette boat.

With one hand pressed to the wheel, Castor turned and fired at Archer, peppering the dock. Archer fell to the pier as the second boat's captain was shot in the arm. He jumped from the boat into the water as the bullets flew. The engine was still running.

Hurtling into the boat, Archer revved it and was off. When the boat's speed peaked, Archer steadied the gun and aimed at Castor's head. The bullet entered just above Castor's shoulder, and, for a moment, he slumped at the wheel. Archer fired again and missed before Castor straightened up and turned the Uzi on him.

Archer ducked under the wheel as the windshield was shattered. He crouched to steer as both craft charged toward a fishing boat cruising toward shore. Castor turned his boat sharply, but rammed the fishing boat's stern, sending both boats spinning. With a jerk, Archer veered to the left of the fishing boat, but was unable to avoid a sideswipe. His boat raced on its side, rose into the air, then smashed with a side-puncturing crunch into Castor's already-damaged craft. Castor floored the pedal and his boat started off again slowly, as Archer brought his boat around to continue the pursuit.

Archer caught up to Castor's badly damaged craft quite easily, and the two boats raced parallel to one another. At point-blank range, the men readied to blast each other. Castor smiled aggressively, baring his teeth as he squeezed the trigger, but at the low speed his boat could muster, a sudden wave caused it to change direction. Archer could almost reach for the end of the Uzi and yank it away. The boats were too close, and they scraped against each other, hard, as they zipped into a swell. Both men toppled. When Archer lurched up, his hopes soared as he recognized an approaching craft as a police boat.

Somehow the police cruiser got between the two antagonists, and their boats circled each other around the slower police craft. Castor riddled the crew with bullets. Taking advantage of the situation, Archer caught up to Castor's boat, which was already taking on water, and rammed his enemy's craft. Archer noticed an oil barge heading for harbor and got an idea—he was feeling his luck again, and his adrenal glands, which had been taxed so many times during the last few days, were kicking in once more. Archer felt strong all over as he steered the linked boats toward the oil barge.

Castor understood what Archer intended. What he didn't realize was that Archer had left his boat and jumped onto Castor's. The abandoned boat, freed of its load, veered hard into the oil barge and crumpled before it exploded into flames. Castor was heading dangerously close to the burning debris. He swerved wildly, spilling Archer over the side. Somehow Archer managed to grab the boat and hold on tight. Castor, meanwhile, grabbed the Uzi's replacement clip and reloaded.

He looked back to find Archer, but didn't see him. Castor searched the surrounding waters as the boat slowed. It was quiet except for the purr of the motor and the gentle lapping of waves. Suddenly, the boat's front dipped. Castor turned just in time to see Archer emerging from the sea in a great gush of white water, pulling himself onto the prow and taking a flying leap. Castor fired, but Archer had already crashed on top of him, and the gun slid across the deck. Archer crawled to it quickly, pulled it into his arms, and pivoted to finish Castor Troy.

But Castor had found the anchor. He was hurling it over his head as Archer moved to get into firing position. The anchor flew out with a sickening crunch into Archer's chin, flattening him. The Uzi flipped up and away behind Archer, but Castor could not tell where it had gone. Unable to find the gun, Castor sprang like a puma at Archer, and, in an instant, had the rope around his neck.

Wrapping the rope tightly around his wrists, Castor jerked it taut and strained with all his might. Archer's face turned a violet-gray as he battled for precious breath. His body spasmed, and his head lodged against the gas pedal—the boat started to pick up speed again.

Castor pulled tighter, as Archer's legs kicked. The boat was racing faster, lurching over the waves. Castor, intent only on strangling Archer, was oblivious to the direction of the boat, not realizing that it was speeding toward shore.

As Castor continued to tighten his grip, Archer could feel his life leaving him. His dying brain buzzed with a thousand black bees, and, then . . . there was silence. Archer knew he was dead. His foot was set at the fabled tunnel of light. He saw his grandparents, his childhood dogs, and . . . Mikey.

Then the boat crashed. It smashed prow first into the rocks of the breakwater, turned over on itself, and dumped the men hard. As Archer hit the rocks, he was very much alive, very much in pain. He sucked air back into his lungs, and his energy surged. Castor had taken a harder hit. The wind was knocked out of him. Dazed and immobile, it was his turn to struggle for oxygen. His lungs would not inflate. He flailed his arms and panicked before the first short breaths returned.

Archer crawled out from under the boat and saw the Uzi lying on the breakwater. It had been lodged behind the life preservers. Castor's head was bleeding as he lifted it from the rocks. He realized he was under the upended boat, crawled out, and sighted the Uzi. It took him but a moment to realize that Archer was up and going for the gun. Castor crawled faster, but stumbled in the gaps of the pilings.

Archer got to the Uzi first. On wobbly legs, he pulled it into his side and stared into his creeping enemy's dilating eyes. For the first time ever, Archer saw fear in Castor Troy. He slowly stood, like a baby who was tremulous at taking his first steps. Castor's body shook with pain. He had to play for time, had to pull one more miracle out of his ass.

"You won't shoot me, Sean," he uttered in weak tones. "I'm unarmed."

Archer discreetly made sure his footing was firm. He listened to the crash of waves against the breakwater, felt cool sea spray on his face. He took the briefest glance at the spectacular clouds floating in a sky as blue as a peacock's breast—for a moment, he imagined he saw his son riding a winged unicorn. Michael was looking down, as Archer's finger rubbed the trigger.

"Okay . . . I have a confession to make," Archer said. "But you aren't gonna like it."

Castor had a rising sense of hope when he saw Archer's arms relax, no longer aiming the gun.

"You're right, Castor. I won't shoot you," Archer said, his eyes unblinking and cold. "Not in the face, anyway."

Sean Archer fired into Castor Troy's chest with the Uzi automatic weapon. Eight bullets flew in the short burst. Three bullets entered Castor's chest, one of them entering his left lung. He jerked and reeled and dropped to his knees in utter disbelief, fell forward, and was still. Archer heard his own breathing, as loud as a hurricane, and watched his nemesis expire.

Sean almost laughed, almost sighed, as he lowered his gun. An FBI chopper approached. He turned to wave at the helicopter, and relief was washing over him like a cool summer rain. But when he turned back to Castor, he saw that he was gone.

Castor was not dead, but he was dying. He was crawling like a slug, leaving a trail of blood on the rocks. He reached the flipped boat's spinning stabilizer screw. The stabilizer's blades were whirring like a buzz saw as Castor taunted Archer.

"It'll never be over, Sean. Every time you look in the mirror, you'll see my face." Castor let his face fall toward the blades as Archer took a springing leap and jerked Castor aside—only his cheek was nicked. Castor was still struggling, pulling up and into the blades.

Archer saw the anchor's rope dangling over the boat's side. He flipped the anchor into the blades. The screw was eating the rope until the anchor yanked up and jammed the mechanism. Castor fell forward into the still blades, then collapsed. His eyes were blank and unmoving. Archer stared at him and blinked. He poked at the lifeless body and kicked it to be sure. Sunlight glinted on the wedding band.

He reached for the ring and tugged it. Just as he was pulling it off, Castor lurched and grabbed his wrist. Archer screamed and bolted backward. Castor smirked and fell lifeless again.

Walking backward, Archer's eyes were glued to his enemy. Was he really dead? He picked up the Uzi and waited, waited for Castor to resurrect. Archer slowly approached and pulled off Castor's shirt to look at the gun wounds. They had stopped bleeding. Perhaps Castor Troy was most sincerely dead.

Archer hoisted the corpse up to the hovering chopper, passing it up to Buzz and Wanda. "Watch the face," Archer said. Buzz yanked the corpse inside, then looked at Archer with concern.

"You okay, Sean?" Buzz asked.

"What did you call me?"

"He called you 'Sean,' Sean," said Wanda, extending an arm to Archer and pulling him inside. She saw him smile his fullest, his long-lost smile, and thought it made the face of Castor Troy almost sweet-looking.

As the chopper flew through the canyons of clouds, Archer thought he saw his son again. The unicorn was resting, chewing on a cloud. Mikey saw his father and waved. The boy no longer had a red balloon, but an all-day sucker. "Good-bye, Daddy," he said, mouthing the words so Archer could read them. "Good-bye, Mikey," Archer mouthed back and waved. Archer was crying now as he watched the unicorn turn tail and his son disappear in the mists. Buzz and Wanda looked at Archer as tears spilled over his cheeks. They looked out the window and wondered what he was waving at.

The sun was setting when the copter landed. Archer had collapsed. He was lifted onto a gurney by a Bureau med-team and rolled into a medevac chopper. Castor's inert body was strapped to a gurney and rolled in next to him. Archer's heart beat faster when he saw he would be alone with the corpse. He reached over and poked the cooling flesh. Eve poked her head in, and he smiled.

"Hang on, Sean. They're bringing their top surgical teams to DC."

"How is he?" Archer asked, jerking his head toward Castor.

"No signs at all," she said with a gentle laugh. "He's a turnip."

"That's what they always say," Archer said, fading, then passing out. Wanda jumped in the copter and Eve followed her on board.

"Eve, I'm sorry. You can't come," Wanda said.

"I'm coming. He's my husband," she insisted, folding her arms.

"No. I'm sorry."

"I'm *not* leaving him."

Eve had crumpled now, was weeping, and sat at the end of the cabin. Wanda walked slowly to Eve, offered a hand. "I know he's your husband. But he works for us. C'mon, I'll have Buzz take you home."

Eve saw that Wanda was stuck and would

have helped her if she could. Jamie looked confused as her mother left the helicopter. She was getting both angry and weepy when Jamie took her hand.

"Mom, will Dad be Dad again?"

"I hope so, honey."

The medevac chopper lifted off. When it was silent, Jamie spoke up. "And you guys say *my* life is screwed up."

Eve put an arm around her daughter, and they walked off with Buzz to his car. Jamie allowed herself to fall into her mother's embrace, as if she were a little girl again.

Walsh's computer system had been linked to the Bureau's mainframe in Washington. Some of his highly experimental techniques had been retrieved, and the world's top surgeons were flown in. When they learned of Archer's story, they were incredulous, then astonished, then delighted when they were asked to take part in the reversal.

What had taken Walsh a relatively short time to do took several weeks to undo. Archer's face had been stripped from Castor's corpse and kept at absolute zero. Archer was made aware that the odds were against him, and if the graft of his old face did not take, he would have to take a donation from a recently expired patient—there was never any question of his keeping Castor Troy's face. Sean asked them to return the bullet scar to his chest—Castor Troy might have been defeated, but what he had done could never be erased, should never be forgotten.

The president of the United States was briefed on the strangest episode in the history of the FBI. He visited Archer before he went under the lasers. "I'm honored, Mr. President," Archer said. "But I have something I need to tell you. Our Constitution is supposed to protect us from cruel and unusual punishment. However . . ."

The president had known about Erewhon prison. It was conceived, constructed, and financed during the last administration. But the current president was utterly shocked to learn of the conditions at Erewhon. Red Walton, the guards, and the bioengineers of the Desiccation Ward were arrested and made prisoners of the complex until their trials. The desiccated inmates were immediately released from the pods and rehydrated. It was learned that their bodies had been used as hosts for certain mutated viruses, and their altered fluids processed for a number of biological products reputed to cure the incurable. The products were sold at an enormous profit to the very wealthy and the very sick in the black markets of Hong Kong and Japan.

Archer was released earlier than anticipated and flown directly from Washington to the Los Angeles office to be debriefed. He walked through the bullpen that morning wearing a contagious grin. He welcomed the applause of his team, and though it was ten o'clock in the morning, he opened and poured a magnum of champagne he had brought with him. Some questioned if it was really Archer. To a few, he was a guy they were once familiar with, a man who had existed without an archenemy.

Archer offered a gift of Godiva chocolates to Miss Brewster (she asked him to call her Kim), and he played music on his office radio. He looked around and thought his space needed some sprucing up, maybe some paintings and plants. But coming from his own desk was a very bad smell. He looked through the drawers and found nothing. What was it? Pyew!

While he waited to be debriefed, he set about making amends. He arranged for Adam Hassler to be adopted by a South Dakota rancher and his wife. Archer hired Gonzalez and Sons to do his own yard. He made sure their truck had been returned and that they had been reimbursed for their losses. Archer sent a generous check to the men's shelter of St. Vincent de Paul and a hundred roses to Ruthe.

He had a few other things to get to, but

first he had to find the source of that stink—he couldn't stand it another minute. Getting on hands and knees, he sniffed the stench to a matchbox taped to the underside of his desk. Inside the box was a rotting human something, obviously cut from a long-dead cadaver. A small note read, "Eat this, Sean Cocksucker." The sender of this gift would forever remain a mystery. Archer dismissed it as something left for his dead adversary. And then he laughed about it.

As dusk fell, Eve sat at the dining-room table, trying to catch up on reports, but her mind was someplace else. She heard a car approach and its door open. A man's silhouette was at the front screen door.

"Hi, Eve," the man said, and the voice was her husband's.

Her pulse pounding, she ran to the door and saw his face. When she studied his smile, she burst into tears. It was the most beautiful smile she had ever seen on the handsomest face she would ever know. She sank into his arms and merged into his chest. Jamie stepped out of her room.

"Daddy?"

"Yes. It's me."

"I'm sorry I shot you, Daddy. Am I grounded?" Jamie was crying. She needed her father and ran into his arms. He hugged her, then looked at her face, free of makeup.

"Just don't do it again," he said, and chuckled. Eve was warmed to hear him laugh.

"I got a promotion, Eve," he told her. "I'm going to be West Coast Director. It's a desk job."

"Really?" she asked.

"Really. I want my life back," he said, brushing away her tears. Jamie stared at her parents. She had never imagined they were this much in love.

"You know what I want?" Eve asked.

"What?" Archer whispered, and felt himself growing.

"A good night's sleep."

Sean Archer embraced his wife and kissed her mouth with his own lips.

ACKNOWLEDGEMENTS

We are indebted to John Woo for his vast experience and creativity with us. We are much richer for his generosity.

Thanks to John Travolta, Nicolas Cage, and our phenomenal cast for their vivid contributions to their characters, many of which are reflected in this book.

We are grateful to Sherry Lansing and Paramount Pictures, to Micheal Douglas, Steve Reuther, Terence Chang, Jonathan Krane, David Permut, and Mike Simpson for their support; and to John Goldwyn, Tom Levine, Brian Roskam, Kevin Messick, Dena Fischer, Nana Greenwald, John Schimmel, and Caitlin Blasdell for their hard work on *Face/Off's* behalf.

Thanks to our representatives Peter Nelson, Devra Lieb, and the William Morris Agency "angels," Dodie Gold, Sophy Holonik, and Carol Yumkas for their kindness and endless toil.

Thanks also to our UCLA writing instructors, Bill Froug, Gary Gardner, Lew Hunter, Howard Suber, Richard Walter, and Cynthia Whitcomb, for their help both past and present.

Thanks to our families and friends for their love, encouragement, and patience during our seven-year struggle to bring *Face/Off* to life.

And finally . . . our undying gratitude to Clark Carlton for his imaginative work restoring and expanding in print what could not be done on film.

—Mike Werb & Michael Colleary